VAMPIRES DON'T DRINK WHISKEY

NEW BEGINNINGS NOVELLA

BOOK 2.6

KASHEL CHAR

CONTENTS

Title: Vampires Don't Drink Whiskey: New Beginnings
Novella 2.6

Draft to Digital Paperback ISBN 978-1-998713-10-3

Draft to Digital ebook: ISBN 978-1-998713-11-0

Publisher: Koda Calmz Publishing

Copy Editor: Teresa Fornoff

WARNING

or assume responsibility for author or third-party websites, blogs, critiques, or their content.

This story contains explicit, graphic depictions of gay sex and crude language unsuitable for young or sensitive readers or anyone offended by gay sex.

DEAR READER/LISTENER

THIS BOOK HAS BEEN REVISED FROM A THIRD-PERSON TO A first-person point of view, allowing readers to fully appreciate Juandre and Andrew's journey to becoming the first vampires. New chapters were added to flow better into the New Beginnings Series.

I added a timeline at the end of the book for readers who want to figure out what the fuck had happened and when in chronological order. It contains spoilers and is hidden to avoid revealing too much.

Love to all creatures,
Kashel Char.

CHAPTER I
ANDREW

2014 A.D.

Lexington, Kentucky
United States of America

Kentucky in the summer wasn't for the faint of heart. The heat and humidity were bloody oppressive, even at night. I had just woken up sticky from sweating and hastily headed to the basement gym. Groggy, sleepy, and depressed as usual, I dove into the half-size Olympic swimming pool for my nightly swim. The pool area was dark, and the moonlight cut straight lines through it, disappearing in the maelstrom of water and my drowning thoughts.

I'd dreamed of him again. Now, if I'd known that Juandre would haunt my thoughts day and night for the past ten years, I would never have fucked the man. I couldn't dispute my incisors had prickled at the sexy Hispanic ever since he'd pulled over and smiled a cheeky smile at me. As if I couldn't already read into that, I knew what he would ask me even before he asked. The thing was, I had felt a little peckish and hoped a meal would stop and take me home with him for the night. Prolonging my hunger was never good; my freedom had ended, and I now had to face the organization—the Disciples of the Anunnaki.

That final night of debauchery and discovery was the last item on my list to check off before my year-long sabbatical to clear my head and decide whether I wanted to run away or dismantle the Disciples.

Over the years, I had managed to surround myself with them, and only Tony and the few men in our inner circle knew the true reason for Lord Andrew Whiskey. My board of directors were corrupt men, and by keeping them close, we've been able to monitor their influence in America and worldwide.

The day I announced to the board of directors that I was taking leave, the Vice President seemed ecstatic enough for me to pack my bags and leave to find my purpose. The fucker even waved me off, smiling.

En route to the airport, I changed my mind. At first, I wanted to leave and never return, but the answer came to me through a billboard advertisement for RVs. It said; *Discover North America and experience freedom.* I was only a few miles from the estate's driveway when I asked the taxi driver to stop and drop me off in front of the enormous billboard. I grabbed my bags and sent the taxi man on his way. Beneath the billboard and the stars, I draped my suit jacket over my suitcase and used it as a pillow while I lay in the grass, looking up at the people smiling around a campfire with the RV in the back. It called to me to do that, and I knew some things in life just needed to be done, no matter how stupid it looked or sounded to others. Clearing my troubled mind, I lay back, looking at the happy, carefree scene and wondering if it was real. I remember asking myself if people could indeed be happy by just living on the road.

Then I dozed off, dreamed about being barefoot, and woke up still dressed in my blue Armani suit. People laughed at me, pointing to my feet. A man even asked, "Are you planning to hike barefoot? Don't you think you need shoes?" I remembered thinking runners wouldn't match the suit and that I should unpack my bag and put on jeans and a T-shirt, and then the man said, "Yes, that's better. Now go find your freedom."

When I woke up, I grabbed my leather sling bag, stuffed it with socks and the bare necessities, left the rest of my bags out of sight, and started hitchhiking through the United States, up to Canada, and back again.

Leaving the world I knew behind me put everything in perspective. Although I had stayed in touch with my best friend, everyone else had thought I was backpacking through Europe. I thought it sounded classier than hitchhiking through North America.

It was my last stretch home when a ride had pulled up and the driver had made a deal I couldn't resist. I'd been offered many rides and been made just as many offers from bored homemakers to truckers, but when Juandre had pulled up next to me, I just knew I had to fuck him. Juandre, with his perfectly combed dark hair and aristocratic flair of superiority. The young man instantly impressed me, and when we locked gazes, something inside me clicked like it was meant to be, so I shut up and played along. Usually, I would drink my fill, implant a thought that they were tired, and had pulled over to rest, then they woke up, I would be miles away. But something magnetically drew me to the inno-cent, yet hopeful, flamboyant young man.

At first, he seemed to be Mommy's rich bratty boy who had all the money to solve all his problems. Little did he know who and what I was and that, although I was a billionaire, I had never thought happiness and love could be bought. For my amuse-ment, I had decided to play along. Even though I was tired and hungry, it had pissed me off that Juandre had taken one look at me and judged me by my appearance. He had thought I was poor, unedu-cated, and down on my luck, so I gave the kid his fantasy.

Reading his mind, I discovered he lied about his name, so I gave Juandre the impression that I was also someone else. I'd told him I was married and had one boy but that my wife and I were too poor to send him to university. In fact, I was a whiskey tycoon from Lexington, Kentucky, not fully human. I was born in Germany, in one of Hitler's experimen-tation camps, where they tried to create the perfect superhuman, but in 1968, I was bitten and infected by an Anunnaki, which made me some kind of new species, like the Anunnaki. But something different.

Over the years, I discovered I had abilities that no ordinary human possessed. I knew I needed to drink blood to stay alive, and I discovered I could alter my appearance, but by the end of that weekend we spent together, I had forgone cloaking myself and selfishly wanted him to remember me, so I never wiped his memory.

I certainly wasn't planning on marrying a woman, and since gay marriages weren't legal in Kentucky, marriage was something other idiots did, not me. I had a 1 closeted don't fuck with me persona in the boardroom, and I knew I would lose credibility and be voted out of my own company before returning from my honeymoon. The world was full of people with different stories, tastes, and backgrounds, but most of all, different types of bodies and uncountable ways to fuck and get fucked.

Still, I kept seeing those dark brown eyes looking down at me with love in my dreams.

I'd been obsessively thinking about the cheeky Juandre, not Sam, as he lied and had told me without batting an eyelash. The vision of him smiling or how he crooked his neck to see out of the car when our gazes met for the first time when he offered me a ride, for a ride. Maybe it was his jugular throbbing, or how he looked up at me through his neatly combed chocolate brown bangs, or the clean whiff of soap and cologne when he shook his head. Maybe it was hunger and not lust, but that stern look on his face when he asked me if he could blow me—the anticipation in his chocolate-brown eyes. Like a naughty kid asking Santa for a gift, half expecting to hear bad news but hoping for the best.

I've never forgotten the same vulnerable look when he entered me from behind, the vulnerability and trust we had shared near the end of the weekend. Our true selves had shone but were dulled by the false facades and small lies about his reality of being happy, rich, and spoiled. He had believed he was rotten in his core and that his *kink* and dirty secrets weren't beautiful. But in those few hours, we had fit perfectly, understanding the power exchange —the giving and taking. Learning and surrendering. Affirming and acknowledging each other as a perfect union existed in those moments. We both yearned for a closeness and togetherness we weren't allowed to have in our real lives. Certainly not forever.

When Juandre started with the boy and Daddy games? God, that had revved my motor. Pedal to the metal, he burned my exhaust pipe bright white and opened the door to a kink I had never imagined I would crave. Switching roles excited and confused me, and I had fucking loved it. I shivered; the fleeting thoughts vibrated my insides as I quivered for the sexy Hispanic. My band-aid for missing and yearning for his touch was as useless as throwing a pebble on a geyser and expecting it to miraculously plug the hole.

The problem with my first aid solution was that by the time I'd lined someone up at kink clubs or online hookups, my mood had deflated. It felt like a big fishhook was lodged in my heart, pulling me in the opposite direction towards *him*. I truly wanted to relive the whole weekend, the whole package. Not just pieces of it. I desired the entire magical moment from when Juandre stopped his little sports car at the side of the road until I climbed into the taxi to pretend I was flying home.

Asking a man to re-enact it was silly, and by the time I'd explained what I needed, I could have fucked this trick twice and had dinner. After one try, I'd given up.

That unforgettable weekend gave me the strength to go home and pick up the pieces of my life. Manage the business with a determination to carry my promise through. But every so often, I reminisced about that weekend. Like today, as I swam like an Olympic freestyle swimmer and my body sliced through the lukewarm water I wondered what Juandre was doing. The sloshing and kicking dulled the world around me, leaving me alone to enjoy my thoughts and memories about him.

Did he marry the girl his family wanted, or had he decided to come out with the truth? Had he continued his studies and become a doctor practicing medicine? Where was he doing that? I wondered whether Juandre was happy and whether he even thought about me. Had he gone looking for the man he'd bought a plane ticket for, only to find the man he had fucked didn't exist?

I finally decided to do one last tumble turn and kicked myself as hard as possible off the wall and drifted to the opposite side, which was eighty-two feet away, without kicking or using my hands— something I ritually did as I enjoyed floating while the momentum took me to where the stairs were and I exited the pool. I wrapped an extra-large terry cloth towel around my waist and went to the private ensuite of my bedroom to get dressed for work. After a quick shower, I hastily dressed in the crisp, freshly laundered powder blue button-up shirt and only the trousers of the black *Armani* suit my dutiful friend and butler, Tony Alonzo, daily hung ready for me after my swim.

Preferring to walk barefoot in my space, I left the socks and shoes for later. If I were called to a meeting or had an appointment, I would wear my slip-ons, loafers, or flip-flops, depending on the weather or how important the meeting was. I liked dressing smart but casually, making a statement with my footwear that the boardroom culture didn't restrict me, nor would I ever wear uncomfortable shoes to impress people. That was one thing I'd learned on my travels. Shoes were important, yet they needed to serve their purpose.

Sitting behind my desk, I struggled to think about anything else. I bent down and ruffled in my desk's lower drawer, where I had hidden Juandre's number and the other small trinkets I'd collected during my travels. Nothing big, nothing too heavy I couldn't carry in my backpack. Things like key rings, postcards, or something small like a bottle cap from when I drank a beer on Cannon Beach in Washington.

"Would he even recognize me? I'm just a man he'd given a ride and had taken to a hotel to fuck. For fuck's sake, Andrew, it's been ten years," I said softly to myself. Frustrated with myself, I slammed the drawer closed. "I've had enough. I must find him. I need to know if he feels the same about me."

I looked at the little piece of paper in my hand. I'd looked at it many times and, after ten years, the numbers had faded on the yellowed paper.

He'll be in his early thirties, and I'll still look exactly like I did ten years ago. Will he even remember me? Would he stir indignation against the world he now lived in, or would he accept himself even with the false background he'd painted? Would he utterly disregard himself as a gay man, and be the opposite of the man he'd led me to believe he was?

I was tired of wondering. Over the last ten years, I had constantly weighed the pros and cons of whether to phone and have an honest conversation or pretend to be the human fantasy man Juandre had thought I was. While I had lied then, I wouldn't be able to maintain the lie now. I whirled my mind numb in circles, wondering what to do and whether it was even worth it.

Maybe the reality of what truly happened was only my imagination, but I needed to find out. Was it real or not? Otherwise, I'd spend eternity wondering *what if*, just as I've done these past ten years. *What if I'm throwing my last chance away?* Damnit, I had to know!

With my mind finally made up, I leaned over to call Tony, my assistant extraordinaire.

"Tony, I think it's time to do your thing," I said.

I heard a loud "Yes!" as if Tony had muffled the phone and forgot I could hear him through the office door.

CHAPTER 2
JUANDRE

2014 A.D.

Lexington, Kentucky

United States of America

It was Saturday afternoon when I finished my shift at the Lexington Trauma and Burn unit. I looked forward to coming home and relaxing with my son, Charlie. Charlie had just turned ten, and all he wanted for a birthday gift was one day alone with me. His request was a shocking awakening, and I had promised Charlie that this weekend would be his alone.

Arriving home, I switched off my phone. I had promised my son it was our weekend, and I planned to make the most of it. I planned to explain how and why his mother and I had divorced.

We talked in between swimming and relaxing next to the pool. When we finally ran out of something cold to drink, I got up to get something to eat and drink. "I'll be right back. I must use the washroom and bring something to enjoy next to the pool."

"Okay, Dad, I'll time you," Charlie said like my father used to say when encouraging speed. *Let's see how fast you can run and grab this or that for Daddy.* The results were amazing each time.

After the divorce, my relationship with Charlie wasn't great. His mother had filled his head with hateful and negative comments about my sexuality, and how I identified myself didn't help either. Lately though, my son and I have gotten comfortable with each other. After telling him about myself, he seemed to understand now that it wasn't his fault and that there was no way his mother and I would ever get together again.

Charlie was old enough for a mature versus preteen conversation, so I was going to use the time to have a good talk and explain everything from my perspective, as I knew Charlie's mom had done her best to make me sound like the villain.

During our swim today, I explained to Charlie who I was and what I thought I was, saying that I was still discovering myself after a lifetime of wearing a mask to please others like my ex-wife and parents. While I told him I liked to wear makeup and lipstick, I had decided to keep the silk underwear for talks after his number eighteen birthday. I told him I liked men but hadn't found anyone special yet and that I'd introduce Charlie to that man when I did. I said I wanted the freedom to wear flamboyant clothing at work or home on certain days. All day, or not. The choice should be mine, as Charlie likes to choose his own clothing.

We'd touched on the "drag queen" subject and what it meant to me. To me it was all about putting on feminine clothing, a costume from a particular era and then performing in it. I told Charlie it was also about flamboyance, acting, and singing. Charlie understood my cheerful nature. Plus, the kid had ears. Whenever he heard me, Charlie told me I sing like a nightingale, especially when I sang lullabies or felt happy and goofy. I was naturally playful, and Charlie understood that drag was all that but just for adults. Some women liked to do it, too, and they were called kings instead of queens.

Charlie liked that a lot.

He also knew that although it was usually viewed as an art form, I wanted to embrace it fully.

Knowing myself, though, that would mean that one day I'd like to wear a pencil skirt and high heels, while the next day I'd love to wear my pink Dr. Martins ankle boots with black stretched denim, accessorized with a flashing pink handbag. I was beginning to explore my options. One thing was for sure, I loved feeling like a beautiful butterfly.

I'd also told Charlie how I had been forced into marrying his mother, and it made my day when Charlie answered that she was acting like a bitch— his words. Of course, I had had to reprimand the little dude for speaking that way, but deep down, having someone in my corner for a change felt amazing. That also explained why I didn't like talking to Grandmommy or Grandpappy.

While I'd explained that his mother and I had been family friends growing up together, that we both had gotten accepted at Vanderbilt, where we had stayed friends and study partners, I *hadn't told him* that one night we'd gotten extremely wasted, and I had somehow gotten her pregnant, that I have never remembered how, or the mechanics thereof. *God, how had she gotten me to ejaculate? Nor had I told him* that she most probably dosed me up and that I'd objected furiously to being the father, but my parents and she had had the umbilical cord blood tested to determine DNA paternity, and, yes, I was the pappy.

We married before Charlie was born, and I saw her less after. She only wanted to know if she could get me to marry her. I never touched her again. We had jobs, but she was more interested in hanging out with her friends and colleagues than me. We just stopped talking—no deep conversations and certainly no playful teasing.

I grabbed my phone off the fridge, where I'd hidden it from myself earlier and switched it on to check my messages, only to have Charlie yell from outside, "Dad, you promised no phone. Remember, this weekend is ours!" I jumped with surprise, caught in the act.

Damn, kid, I swear you have X-ray eyes.

"No, no! Not for work, this is for fun, for us, Daddy-promise," I shouted and fumbled to find the music app to play my favorite playlist—the one I'd created after that incredible weekend with Ryan. While Ryan had been my first and definitely hadn't been my last, he featured every night in my wet dreams. I guessed it was true about a man's first; you never forgot them. I loved cheesy and was besotted with the idea of lip-syncing, especially to that catchy hitchhiking song by *Heart*; *All I Want to*

Do is Make Love to You because it reminded me of Ryan.

I switched my phone to its loudest setting and started preparing lunch for us. My swim trunks dripped water on the terracotta tiles. I grabbed my towel and shimmied it with my bare feet. The rhythm of the music always carried me to that night. I relaxed for the first time in a long time and let go of my inhibitions.

I let go and sang at the top of my lungs, "One night of love, was all we knew... all I want to do is make love to you." I closed my eyes and danced to "our" song, my secret song for Ryan and me, not caring about work or anything else.

My talk with Charlie went well, and I felt free to do what I liked. I swayed my hips to the music as I dove into the fridge, searching for cheese and tomatoes. I raised my hands and waved the loaf of bread around. I knew I must have looked idiotic, but I loved it. I loved feeling free in my skin, and performing had always been my dream. Feeling elated and happier than I'd felt in a long time, and because I knew every word by heart, I sang along, and as I hit the chorus, I let go. I swiveled around, thrusting my hips wildly, bellowing the lyrics into the French loaf in one hand pretending it was a microphone.

Then I opened my eyes and jerked to a halt. "Oh, my dear lord!" I yelped, my effeminate lilt pronounced when the song ended. A silhouette of a tall man filled the doorway. I squinted, judging by the man's expression, he'd been there a while. "Motherfucker, who are you? How the hell did you get in here!"

Before he answered, I hopped back with fright and searched for a weapon. I grabbed the only thing I could find and pointed the bread at him. "Are you real?" I asked because it looked like a ghost was standing in my doorway. The man smiled wide, showing a perfect set of teeth. Visions flipped like a movie preview through my mind, and I froze. That smile was the exact same smile I saw in my dreams or when I fucked my hand.

I stood there, frozen, holding my elbow with one hand and the other covering my mouth with the bread. Surprised for several reasons, but mainly because he looked the same as when I'd sent him on his way in a taxi ten years ago. *He must be a manifestation.*

The man I used to call country-man threw his head back and laughed. My spine snapped straight.

That seemed to amuse him even more. I tried to play it cool like he hadn't just caught me dancing and singing like a crazy idiot.

"Ah... um," I stammered and dove for my phone as the next embarrassing song started. It was Ryan, and he chuckled like a big, happy giant. The melodic sound and a pleasant aura filled the spacious kitchen.

Open-mouthed, I stood there and looked at him. Ryan's hands rested casually on the sides of the door frame, his expression was one of delighted amusement, but then he blinked it away and straightened. He wore dark blue jeans and a white button-up shirt that stretched snugly over his chest and enfolded well-developed biceps. Our gazes locked. His green eyes sparkled, reflecting the sunlight escaping over his shoulders while his big, muscled frame blocked the doorframe.

Maybe I slipped and fell and cracked my head open.

"Dad, what's taking so long? Who are you talking to?" Charlie asked, trying to push Ryan aggressively to the side. I was still in shock, but it seemed Ryan knew what to do in a situation like this. He kneeled at Charlie's height and held out his hand.

"Hello. My name is Andrew," he said. Charlie reluctantly grabbed his hand, and they shook.

Hmmm, did he just introduce himself as Andrew?

Charlie folded his arms and lifted his chin. "Hi, nice to meet you. But if you're here to take my dad to work, it's my weekend. You can go. He'll see you on Monday. At work," Charlie said and moved his hands to his hips.

Ryan—no, not Ryan, but Andrew, laughed. The deep timbre of his voice rumbled and rolled through me just like I remembered. I tilted my head to the side and took another long look at him. *He's aged well. He must be almost fifty years old but looks younger than me.*

Charlie tapped my arm for attention. "Dad, tell him that this weekend is our weekend. It's your weekend off," Charlie persisted while I recovered from the shock of seeing Ryan. No, *Andrew!*

He must be real because he had talked to Charlie in my kitchen.

"Don't worry," Ryan said. "I'm here to visit, not take your daddy anywhere." He made a big cross over his heart and put his hand flat over it. "I'm here as a friend, just saying hello. I won't steal your time, I promise. I will only watch. Is that okay?"

Charlie looked perplexed, standing there

between the gorgeous man of my dreams, now known as Andrew and me. "I guess, as long as he doesn't have to work."

"Good, and thank you. I promise only fun times. Are you guys swimming?" Andrew asked and got up from kneeling. Damn, he was big and beautiful.

Charlie seemed to relax. "Yes, do you know how to do a handstand underwater? Because I can, but my dad can't."

Andrew regarded Charlie but stole a glance at me every other second. He fiddled with something in his pocket. "I can do a lot of tricks. I love water, and I swim every night," Andrew said. I stood, gobsmacked, watching the two.

"Why do you swim at night? People sleep at night. My dad says it's dangerous to swim at night."

"Yes, it is dangerous, but the sun is even more dangerous for my skin. It burns and dries fast in direct sunlight. See?" Andrew pushed his sleeve up, revealing the marble-white skin I remembered vividly, touching and licking it.

"Oh, that's not good," Charlie said, running his hand over Andrew's arm.

"Yeah, but don't worry, I can do other things when you swim. I'll wait in the shade and watch you do your handstands."

"You can? You will?" I asked without thinking, wondering what those things were and that he'd stay with us, with me. *Fuck, he just got here.* "I meant, you will? Sorry, I meant, please?" I stumbled over my words, looked at the loaf of bread still in my hands, and put it on the counter.

Andrew shrugged. "Why not? I have all the time in the world and want to see his tricks." He wiggled his eyebrows at Charlie and then pinned me with a stare, meaning much more than that.

"Cool," Charlie said, smiling.

And I said, "Cool," because what the fuck else could I say?

CHAPTER 3
ANDREW

IT WAS A LOVELY DAY OUTSIDE, THE SKY FILLED WITH GRAY-white clouds, and I couldn't remember the last time I'd been outside. As beautiful as the day was, I was sitting beneath the scorching sun and dehydrating by the second. I even wondered if I could get out of the chair. I was slowly turning into a mummy, and if I'd sat another hour, the wind would scatter me like a cordless leaf blower.

I forced myself to get up, smile, and say, "Be right back. I need to... uh, go to the loo." My voice was raspy, and my throat felt like sandpaper.

I fell into the house and scrambled for my phone to call Tony. "Hello, sir. Are you ready to go?" Tony answered cheerfully.

"Need blood. Thirsty," I sputtered, barely

finishing my sentence because no air was moving in and out of my lungs. "Bring blood to the washroom window in the back of the house," I said and hung up. Ripping the fridge door nearly off its hinges, I grabbed water, juice, and protein shakes.

Thank fuck, yes!

Arms full of rehydration fluids, I swayed and stumbled down the long hallway. The washroom door was closed. Of course, it was. Using my elbow, I awkwardly opened the door, fell into the guest washroom, and planted myself on the closed toilet lid. With fingers as numb and dry as twigs, I fumbled and struggled to unscrew the lids of the bottles. After deciding it was taking too long, I ripped the lids off and threw the contents down my throat. With my thirst quenched to manageable levels, I felt more coordinated, and my eyeballs felt less like cement.

Why did I do this to myself? Because I still wanted Juandre.

Shaking and graceless, I got up, opened the window and hung my hand out, hoping Tony was already there. I flapped my hand around a few times before I felt the bags handed to me.

Thank fuck!

Hastily, I bit into each bag and sucked them

dry. I could feel my body being restored as Tony whispered outside, "I have more if you need them, sir."

I grabbed the empty bags, stuck my hand out with them, and exchanged the empties for three more full bags. I emptied the first two, and I opened my eyes after sinking my teeth into the last bag. As the fates would have it, Juandre stood pale, wide-eyed, and open-mouthed in the open doorway of the bathroom, looking at me while the sixth bag of blood shriveled in my hand.

Oops!

Juandre flapped his wrists, searching for words. "Please don't say you can explain because you fucking can't. This is not happening, and I didn't see you drink blood like a fucking vampire!" he said through clenched teeth.

I wiped the blood from the corners of my mouth and said, "I'm not—"

"Sir?" Tony interrupted. "Do you need more? I have six more here," he said from outside like a crack dealer. I got up and handed the last three bags out the window. Should I wipe Juandre's memory, or do I let the pieces fall as they may, I asked myself while I gave Tony a hand signal that meant I'm okay, and you may go now.

"Sir?" he asked, not understanding the universal language of thumbs up.

I muttered through clenched teeth, "Thank you, Tony. Please wait in the car. I'll be out directly," I said, feeling life return to my numb limbs. *At least I can run and join Tony waiting in the getaway car if Juandre chases me out.*

Juandre waited, hands on his hips and fear in his eyes.

"C... can we talk?" I stuttered. I was reading Juandre's thoughts. He was busy running through all the possibilities and scenarios, but he ended again at what he thought stood before him and waited, while I waited for my dehydrated brain cells to recuperate and return to firing synapses.

If I were a vampire, I would undoubtedly be the luckiest, but stupidest vampire alive because I wasn't sure if any other fool had lived to see another day after such self-inflicted sun damage. It was probably time to read up on Bram Stoker. If I died and lost all that whiskey, Ish would never forgive me.

Juandre opened his mouth to say something, then abruptly turned on his heel and left the wash-room dramatically.

My heart felt like a piece of cork in my chest, but

as it revived, it sped up and went into tachycardia. I was way past nervous. All my fears from the past ten years were coming true. I didn't know what to do, so I sat on the closed toilet seat and hung my head in my hands.

Colossal fuck-up—ticked, yes.

Plan to ease him into this—ticked, no.

Coax him into it steadily—ticked, no.

Find out if he wanted me—ticked, no, because I'm a fucking idiot!

I had planned this big romantic reveal. I even had a speech written! It wasn't supposed to be like this; it was supposed to be perfect with laughs and rolling naked. Okay, maybe it became a bit of daydreaming, but now I had fucked it all up. *And tied a pretty bow around it—a red bow with blood bags.*

Miserable and hopeless, I sat on the toilet and eventually came out, no pun intended. The house was dark and quiet. Lights flickered in the distance, up the hallway, probably the living room. Like a ninja, I stuck to the wall and snuck closer to see.

Juandre and Charlie watched television. Charlie lay on his side, stretched out on the sofa with his head resting on Juandre's lap. Juandre looked up, straight at me. He was beautiful, and the sassy look he gave me was adorable and scary.

It said don't speak and fuck off or else. I felt my cock stir.

I contemplated wiping his mind and trying again tomorrow, but their father-and-son weekend was special. I could wipe it and say he had had a wonderful day with Charlie, but that felt like stealing and cheating, like I was using my powers to have my way and take Juandre's free will away from him.

"I'm going to go," I whispered, feeling like a scared loser with a boner.

Juandre nodded and lifted an eyebrow. His ax-and-dagger expression didn't change. I removed one of my business cards and the paper of the speech I had written and placed both on the coffee table where Juandre rested his feet. His toes looked delicious—the toenails were neatly clipped and painted with red nail polish. Each big toe had a little ladybug painted on it. My heart puckered, and I begged for mercy with my eyes. But the determined look on Juandre's face told me to leave. I swallowed a whimper but choked out, "Please call when you are ready to talk." I then turned and left before I started sucking on those perfect toes.

CHAPTER 4
JUANDRE

I WAS ONE OF THOSE LUCKY PEOPLE——IF I IGNORED something long enough and didn't think about it, *poof,* it disappeared. Usually, that was how I hid my inner queen identity. I pretended she never existed until I let her out in front of a mirror. Which seldom happened because of fear for losing Charlie in the divorce. No, I drowned myself in my work at the Trauma Unit. I suspected my ex-wife knew where her lace underwear had disappeared to, but it was for a different reason than she'd thought I had it, and I didn't care because, *poof,* it didn't happen.

Only Ryan—not Ryan—Andrew—was a memory I couldn't file, shred, or purge.

It was Sunday morning, and the first thing I thought about when I opened my eyes was that the garbage fucking truck was coming tomorrow. Last night, I had chucked *Count Drac's* business card and the *Dear Juandre* letter in the kitchen trash can. While at it, I also chucked and dumped its contents into the big dumpster down the street from my townhouse complex. Far away from myself so I couldn't ever retrieve it, of course I didn't burn, shred, or flush it as a normal scorned person would. I'd intended to get rid of it and forget about it. That was exactly what I planned to do about the man of my dreams, the guy who sucked O-positive blood out of a bag like a dehydrated endurance athlete— yep, never happened.

After *you-know-who* left, I helped Charlie to bed and cleaned up from the day, and, yes, I might have had a quick look at *you-know-who's* business card. It was black with gold engraving with Lord Andrew Whiskey Distilleries and a telephone number written on it. Unfortunately, I didn't possess a photographic memory. Another characteristic I didn't have was impulse control. I had opened the letter and read the words, *Dear Juandre.* Pissed off at the universe, I had stopped reading and trashed it. I had crumpled it up, discarded my only connection to *you-know-who,* and went to bed. I was unsuccessful at falling asleep.

This morning, while taking a piss, I stared into the bowl of water, which was turning a light yellow. For how long, I didn't know. My mind must have taken a quick break. At least my kidneys were functioning fine. As a doctor, I always checked my piss; whether all doctors did was another thing I didn't know, but maybe I should ask when I was back at work.

Also, I needed to get my head checked to figure out what the fuck was wrong with me as I found myself thinking about dumpster diving. On a Sunday morning. While it was raining. *What's wrong with me?* That thought stayed with me as I dashed out the door and down the street.

I stood knee-deep in the trash, flinging shit over my shoulder. The rain was relentless. Bottles and scary-looking things like tampon applicators started floating around my legs. If the rain continued, I'd be much deeper and covered in bloodborne pathogens. I was sure I just stepped in a bag of kitty litter, meaning Toxoplasmosis in the next five days, or if it was old fish tank gravel, definitely mycobacterium, campylobacter, or just plain roundworm in the brain.

Finally realizing I wouldn't find that damn letter, as my chances of finding it were zero against the hundreds of other diseases I could catch, I looked up to the heavens and wondered who or what could have angered the fates so damn much today. Lightning struck and lit the sky with a blinding light. It would be a beautiful sight if it weren't so damn treacherous. *A lightning storm may not be the safest place to view from inside a giant tin can.* The last thing Charlie needed was for me to die and be sent to live with his mom. He wouldn't survive her.

I swallowed the knot in my throat. Realizing that I was very close to barfing, I hurriedly jumped, grabbed hold of the side, and pulled myself out of the dumpster.

There had to be another way. I could ask Randy, a steady booty call, friend, and only lifeline to the stage and lights. He was a detective by day and the fishiest queen by night. He should be able to help. After all, I'd told Randy about my mystery man.

I nixed that thought almost immediately. While it shouldn't be difficult for Randy to find Andrew, it would humiliate me. No, it shouldn't be difficult for me to find him either. All I had to do was phone the Distilleries and ask for...

Who do I ask for? The CEO? I pretended to phone them. "Hello, you don't know me, but my name is

Juandre and I need to speak to your CEO, Andrew. No, he doesn't expect me, and I don't have an appointment." Yeah, right. I'd seen that not working way too many times. I huffed, then sloshed back up to my home, thinking that calling Randy was the better idea.

Now it made sense why he'd given a fake name. It was because he was a billionaire and CEO of Lord Andrew Whiskey Distilleries. However, I couldn't hold that against him since I had also given him a fake name. "But he's a fucking vampire!" I shouted into the sky. *Who, what, else drinks blood and runs like the wind?*

Nausea and anxiety overpowered my ability to think. I needed a shower, and I needed to phone Randy for help. Plus, Charlie would be up soon.

Once home, I dragged my stinky, heartbroken self into the shower and disinfected. I was sure Randy would like to fuck before I asked him a favor, but I hoped not— I needed a friend. *I'm so stupid, stupid, stupid. I wish I'd read the letter. I'm an idiot!*

Later, after I dropped Charlie off at his mother's, I phoned Randy.

"Hello, sexy," he answered in a deep southern drawl. "You wanna come over?" he asked. He was always up for a hard fuck and ready for me, in and out of drag.

"No, thank you. I need to speak to my momma." That was code for stop slutting and listen to me. "You're the only one I can trust to talk to," I said over the car's Bluetooth speaker system. Randy had always hinted at wanting to be more than kai-kai buddies, so I was sure he would jump at the chance to see more of me.

"Wow, this is a first, honey. You want to visit and talk with clothes on?"

"Yes, and I'm outside your house, so you better say yes."

"Yes, of course!" he squealed with excitement. "I always say you're welcome to come over for a beer or to watch a game with me. You're the one who always had a problem spending time with me."

"You know why. Listen, talk to you in a minute. I'm getting out of the car," I said.

"Fuck, are you really here already?" Randy asked, but I didn't answer as I switched the radio off and got out of my red *Porsche*. Randy's townhouse was nestled in arching shrubs and twining vines of honeysuckle. It smelled sweet and inviting as I approached the back door. It was easier to access through the back and was much more private.

"Fuck, you look horrible. Come in, sit down. Do you want a beer or something cold? It's been stuffy lately. We get dumps of rain to cool us for ten minutes, and then it's gone." Randy didn't wait for a reply; he went into the kitchen, then returned with two ice-cold ones, still talking to me.

"Thank you," I eagerly accepted one and took a big gulp, savoring the bitter-cold taste.

Randy sat down opposite me and waited for me to speak. "Well, go on. What have you done?"

I took a deep breath and hoped this came out correctly. "Where should I start? Wait, what? No, I haven't done anything. Do you remember I told you about the man I picked up next to the road, the older man? I was finishing med school. I was almost twenty-three, and he was about fifteen years older than me. His name was Ryan, but I ended up calling him boy, and he called me Daddy." Randy frowned, not making the connection. "Remember me telling you about the first time I popped my gay cherry? It's been so long now, and I still think about him. Every fucking day and every fucking night, I close my eyes and fall asleep, and I think about him," I told Randy.

"Yeah, I remember you telling me about that. I was jealous. That weekend did sound extremely hot.

That's why I tried to play a little with you like that, but it didn't work for us."

"I remember. Losing your wig mid-fellatio wasn't sexy. We kept laughing each time you called me Daddy. It's just not our thing. I get it. But that's not what I'm here to talk to you about." I took another swig of beer. "Guess who stood in my back doorway yesterday?"

"What doorway? Do you mean your back entrance?" he asked, puzzled.

"No, silly, I should have known you would take it like that. No, get your head out of the gutter. My backdoor to the swimming pool. That doorway." I drew a rectangular doorframe animatedly in the air.

Randy's eyes enlarged. "Your mystery man showed up? No stage lights. No phone calls or texts? How did he know where you lived? Tell me every-thing." Randy moved to the edge of his seat.

"I was making some sandwiches for Charlie and me yesterday. I promised him a day for just us. I was singing and dancing, and I turned around, and there he was. The first thing I noticed was how gorgeous he was. The weird thing was that he looked precisely the same as the last time I saw him. As I stood frozen, shocked, and slack-jawed, he greeted Charlie and promised him he was there to watch and that we should continue swimming. They shook on it that he would wait for us to finish having fun. We swam for maybe an hour, and then he disappeared into the house. I should have known by the way he moved. He moved so fast that I saw only a blurred line, like in the movies. I thought maybe it was the water in my eyes. One fraction of a second from us to inside the house."

Randy frowned deeply, pulling a *what-the-fuck* face.

"I went searching for him. I heard something down the hallway and thought maybe he was sick. I heard moaning as if he was in pain. I knocked and thought he'd heard, so I opened the door. You won't believe..."

Randy waited patiently for me to continue. I wiped my face as if to wipe the scene from my mind and kept my voice steady. "You won't believe what I saw. He wasn't in fucking pain, he was savoring it... he sat on the side of the toilet, suckling blood out of a blood bag like a baby from a bottle."

"What the fuck?" Randy shot out of his chair. "Blood out of a bag?"

"Yeah, like a fucking vampire..." I answered, feeling relieved to say it and realizing it sounded ridiculous.

"No, this can't be, maybe you saw him drinking juice, or something else, I don't know."

"I'm a trauma surgeon. I know exactly what a bag of O-positive looks like."

"So did he cut it open to suck it out, or did he bite into it with his... oh my god, I'm going to get us more beer." Randy collected the empty bottles and exchanged them. He handed me one and sat back down, opening his. "Okay, go on."

"It looked like he bit into them and sucked them dry. He had vampire fangs. I just stood there, and then he got up and gave the empty bags to someone on the other side of the bathroom window. He never saw me. He exchanged the bags for three more and sucked on those. By the time they were shriveled up, he'd noticed me."

"Fucking fuck, what the fuck?"

"I know, right?"

"Am I hearing this right? And what did you do?"

"I just turned around, got Charlie, and watched television because what the fuck else could I do? I've seen *Hotel Transylvania* one, two, and three. There is nothing we can do. He is stronger, faster, and smarter. So I hoped he would disappear and never come back, but he came to us and said he would explain and asked if I wanted to know what was going on. I just nodded and wished him away. He left his business card and a letter for me."

"Did you open it? Read it?"

"Charlie fell asleep on the couch, and I just looked at it and thought, this is easy. I'm gonna chuck it away and forget about it and forget about him, and maybe when I wake up in the morning, it'll be like a bad dream or something I can easily forget, and you know how easy it is for me to forget stuff I want to forget."

"Yeah, you've got an excellent selective memory," Randy said, pointing his bottle at me. "You don't remember popping your nails while topping me."

I chuckled, feeling guilty. I'd almost forgotten that.

"That's why I chucked the business card. I might have seen the name of the business and his name, and you won't believe this! He not only works at Lord fucking Andrew Whiskey Distilleries. He is Lord Andrew! He told Charlie his name was Andrew. When we had that weekend, both of us gave a fake name. He was rough around the edges, and I thought he wasn't a person I would generally associate with. He was gorgeous and still is, but so much more. Fuck, he told me he lived in Louisiana, he'd lost his job, and had a wife and kid back in Louisiana. Now that I think of it, his accent was German," I said as I shook my head in disbelief. "He fucking conned me! I thought I fooled him, but I'm the idiot." I let my head fall into my hands—embarrassed and disappointed.

"Stop your pity party," Ryan said. "Concentrate on the fact that he's a fucking unnatural paranormal species that live off human blood. What the fuck? If he's a vampire, then it doesn't make sense. Vampires don't drink whiskey."

"Well, this vampire does drink whiskey, or I don't know, it sounds like it's his distillery. His name is Andrew, and he's the CEO of Lord Andrew Distilleries."

"Girl, this is one big green booger of a situation. I can't believe what you're telling me," Randy said, jumping up and pacing in front of his sofa couch.

I joined him from across the rectangular glass-top coffee table. "This is fucking weird, yes? I know. The thing is..." I sighed. "I need to find him. I don't know... it's... as weird as it sounds, I need to find him. You won't believe it. I climbed into the dumpster and searched for that letter in the rain. I know. That's how hard up I am. The filth and the tetanus." I shivered, feeling it from the crown of my head and down to my toes. "I was fucking sick with the urge to find him. I need your help. That's why I'm here," I pleaded.

"Yeah?" Randy asked, staring at the carpet. He appeared to be deep in thought.

"Yes, please, I need your help. You need to help me. You're the detective. Can you help me? What should I do? Must I go there, or should I do a stakeout first? You know, in *Hotel Transylvania*—"

"What's with the animated vampires with you? There are much sexier movies out there. Have you ever listened to *Théoden* by Nicholas Bella? Now that's some raw sexy vampire shit. That dude, I'd call Daddy all night long," Randy said dreamily. Obviously already bending over and lubing himself for that vampire.

"Wipe the drool off your chin. If you had a kid, you would understand. You watch what they watch. Whether it's *Elsa* singing *Let It Go* over and over, or lip-syncing with monsters in *Hotel Transylvania*. Randy, please help me. Must I go to him, or should I try to phone him? It feels like we've both been thinking about each other for ten years and now that he's come to find me, it was probably not how he wanted to tell me. I saw the devastated look on his face when he realized I saw him. I think he came

to tell me the truth. I don't know what I should do."
I sat down, rubbing my wrists.

"I know what you should do. You should forget about him," Randy said, jumping to get us a third beer each. "This is, this is not good. You're a doctor, and you're a practical man."

"I know, and honestly, being a doctor doesn't matter to me. I care about Charlie, and I care about finding Andrew. I don't care how it sounds or what it would look like. Or, as stupid as it sounds, my reputation and credibility don't matter. I need to know. Do you understand? It's like I'm obsessed or something."

"Okay. Okay, okay, okay. I'll help you. I think you decided on the safest way forward. It's good you came to me. I'll help you. Don't worry, Momma's got your back. I've told you before that you can come to me for help with anything. So this is you being here for the right reasons. This queen will cover your ass. I'll help you search for him and check this guy out. If he gives you any trouble, I'll fuck him up. He better be a vampire. Otherwise, he's a crazy fuck that drinks blood for fun. He was in your house. If I get a sniff of crazy, he dies," Randy explained, his voice flipping over the high notes the more excited he got, with murderous intent written all over his face. He seemed super eager to come to my rescue. "I'll check him out to see if he's dangerous or legit and if he's a vampire. Then at least, both of us know what we're dealing with."

"Thank you. It's good to know I'm not alone in this." I thanked him earnestly. Randy was my only friend, and he came through for me.

"It could also be me saving you from making headlines." He made air quotations. "Trauma surgeon sells all his belongings to join a weirdo's cult. Sit around the fire and drink blood like vampires."

"Yeah, but you should see him," I said. "He's got this marble-white skin with these stunning deep green eyes. His long incisors make sense now that I think about it. Also, his lustrous blond hair is incredible. You'll see. He'll knock your breath away. I saw his face every time I had a quiet moment for myself for the past ten years. I can't forget about him. Shit!" I slapped a hand over my mouth. "I'm thirty-three years old and sound like a teenager with a crush! I'm sorry, I'll change the subject. But please come with me to the head office. Come support me because, obviously, they'll ask me if I have an appointment."

"Does he know you're coming? How will they call him down to the front door?" Randy asked.

"A walk-in needing to see the CEO. Right, I've seen that too many times not happening in the movies," I said, feeling defeated.

"So you tell them you're Juandre, and Andrew needs to come down and talk to you. Wait, he visited you in the daylight?" Randy rambled and flipped questions faster than *McDonald's* pushed burgers at the drive-through.

"You know what they say about vampires. They can't sit in the sun. They'll burn and turn to dust. Why the fuck was he sitting outside? You need to ask him and let him explain this to you. Where's Charlie?"

"His mum's," I said, suddenly feeling drained of all energy now that I got it all off my chest.

"Good, so we have time. I don't know if the offices will be open today because it's Sunday. Do you want another beer?"

"Yes, please." I liked that Randy only drank non-alcoholic beers.

"It's so hot today," Randy said, his voice muffled inside the fridge. I heard the door shut with a dull thump. Bottle caps clanged into the trash, and then Randy handed me an ice-cold one.

"Hmmm, you know he sat outside in the shade.

Maybe that's why he was in distress," I said to Randy, starting to feel sorry for the idiot.

"It seems so. That is, if he is a vampire. Do you want to go out for dinner?"

"No, thank you. I'm not hungry."

"I'll order some pizza. You can chow if you want. Otherwise, I'll chow alone, but you shouldn't be alone now. Just relax here with me. Just chill out, and we can talk this out."

"Okay. Thank you. You know, you're my best fuck buddy and friend. We do talk most of the time. But this is different. Thank you for listening to me, and thank you for being here with me."

"Yeah, no problem. You know, I've always told you we can go out for a beer or martini and get to know each other better, but you're the one who's always busy with work. I'm always just enough between work and home. I don't mind it now. It hurt initially, but I have my sisters, unlike you. I understand you. I know who you are, and how alone you are, and you preferred it that way."

"I know. I did. I do. I function better if I don't have lots of social responsibilities. For years, all I had to do was go to work, come home, and be with Charlie. That's all I want at this stage, especially now that the divorce is finalized. If Chrissy had found out about me, she would have gotten full custody. No judge would leave a ten-year-old boy with a gay man, especially a drag queen. Anyway, life is less complicated, and I like it. I'm more comfortable and feel in control."

"This isn't because you want Andrew?"

"Oh Lord, what's wrong with me? What am I getting myself into?" I sighed. "I have to... umm... get this behind me and talk to him. Okay?"

Randy got up and ordered pizza. He was a good guy, the sort of man everyone knew and liked. His charismatic personality was what made him most attractive. He was tall and athletically built, average-looking with brown curly hair, big, friendly brown eyes, and the widest smile that never disappeared. I sighed, realizing again that my life would have been less complicated if I had fallen in love with Randy.

After dinner and some research, Randy got a bright idea. "You know what?" he eagerly said to me. "I think we should go scope this place out now. I know where it is. I know the distillery. It sits on an enormous estate just outside Lexington."

I nodded. "Yeah, let's go," I said. "Let's go check it out now." I agreed with Randy that the sooner, the better.

"That's about forty-five minutes to an hour." Randy jumped up, all excited, packing his duffle bag. "Come on, I have clothes for you to wear. We need to wear something dark. And we need ski masks. And maybe we need cameras—maybe rope. Let me think. Knives. Uhm. If it's vampires, absolutely knives. Do we need garlic?"

"Fuck no. I'm not going to wear garlic around my neck. Don't think it works, remember, I fucked him already, and I don't believe the garlic does anything. We had dinner with garlic, now that I think about it."

"Okay, better your neck than mine because I'm not getting my blood sucked. So I'm wearing garlic," Randy said, serious about this mission. A few minutes later, we left. Fifty minutes later, we were at the distillery.

We had arrived at Lord Andrew Distilleries by sundown. The massive building on the estate had blackened windows. No surprise there. The big question was how many vampires were inside. But Randy didn't seem to be worried. He came prepared.

"They won't hurt us if we don't hurt them," Randy whispered while still sitting in his car, checking out our target. If he was wrong, he had the garlic and his knife.

Once out of the car, Randy dropped-rolled and elbow-crept closer, seemingly like a professional. I copied him as best I could as we made our way up to the front of the building.

"Dammit, the front doors are locked," I said, pulling on the doors while Randy watched my six.

"Let's sneak in the back. Maybe someone left the back door open," Randy whispered.

"Why?" I whispered back. "If he's not here, then why try to get inside?" I reasoned with Randy, who looked too inquisitive for this mission and I was having second thoughts. "I don't think it's safe to sneak around a vampire's back entrances," I said, but as soon as I said it, Randy and I giggled like two schoolboys.

Quietly as possible, we snuck to the back. We tried to be quiet, but we kept falling over our feet as we laughed. Darkness covered the earth; the only sounds were cicadas and far-off motor vehicles on the highway. We finally stopped at a wall at the back end of the building.

"Shhht." Randy used hand signals that only a Navy SEAL could understand. I lifted my hands in question.

"Wait here," he whispered, "I'll jump over and signal to you if it's safe, then you can come." We began laughing again. When we stopped long enough to catch our breath, he added, "Stay here." He shot away, turned and ran back, jumped, pulled himself onto the wall, and rolled over by swinging his legs first.

I doubted I could do such a maneuver and hoped Randy unlocked a door for me. It wasn't long before I got the signal and heard a door open with a click and a squeak. Ryan came back and helped me over the wall, then we both made our way to the door. I smelled chlorine the second I stepped through the open doorway, and then felt the high humidity of an indoor swimming pool. Randy gave me a few more indecipherable hand signals I couldn't understand, so I mouthed voicelessly, *what the fuck?*

Oh, Randy was planning to go down to the basement for a lookie-look. I shook my head and tip-toed deeper inside the open-plan gym area. Then I swung left to hide in the locker room while Randy collected vampire intel. I took a few deep breaths, steadying myself, and wondered again what the fuck we were doing here.

Then, a deep voice purred seductively behind me. "Hmmm, hello, Juandre. This is a pleasant surprise."

CHAPTER 5
ANDREW

Lust, love, and infatuation—mix those three and Google it. My face will pop up. With fangs, of course. When I smelled Juandre, my fangs dropped, and my cock got hard. The tantalizing smell unique to him engulfed and consumed me, so no reasoning, only instinct, drove me forward.

We charged toward each other, and our mouths collided. Like two rabid dogs fighting, Juandre planted his lips against mine, rasping his tongue over my incisors and slipping deep into my predatory mouth. The kiss was passionate and aggressive. I withdrew my fangs and went to town on Juandre's deliciously sweet mouth. Passion built, layer upon layer, until we were breathless and dizzy for oxygen.

I stopped the dancing of our tongues for a

second. Weaving my fingers into Juandre's hair, I fisted a handful and pulled his head back. "Why are you sneaking around, Juandre? I told you to phone, and I'd talk to you." I couldn't wait for an answer. I pulled Juandre closer and dove back into kissing that cheeky fucking mouth.

Juandre whined between breaths of air. We found a rhythm; kiss breath question, kiss breath answer, kiss breath question, kiss breath answer.

Juandre seized my hips with eager hands and steered me backward, pressing my naked back against the cold granite tiles on the wall. My thin speedo did nothing to hide my arousal, and I felt my cock head pop up past the elastic and leak pre-cum. I was wild with need and tried to rein in my urge to bite Juandre and make him mine. For a second, we locked gazes as if to confirm each other's presence, and then we brutally attacked each other's mouth again, stopping now and then, heaving a few breaths, and looking at each other. Seeing Juandre's face reassured me that this was real and was genuinely happening. We moaned and clutched fistfuls of hair and skin.

"Why are only my cock and balls out?"

"Don't know, do something about it, boy,"

Juandre said as he squeezed and tugged on my balls. Pleasure zinged through my body.

"Say it again, Daddy," I begged in a low growl into Juandre's mouth. We were being reckless. Anyone could come into the gym, but it was beautiful. I didn't want to spoil the intensity of the moment. The need between us was powerful. It was a thing that never cracked or broke, no matter how far or thin it stretched through time.

Juandre let out soft sigh after soft sigh when I tugged at his shirt and slipped a hand under the hem, resting my fingers on the warm, hard ripple of muscles across his stomach. The sound of his throaty groan shot straight through me.

"Have to have you, please, Daddy," I begged.

"Ah, yes, take me, boy," Juandre answered. "Is it safe here? Can anyone come into the gym?" he asked, out of breath and panting.

"Usually, it's only me using the pool area this time of night," I said as my hips slid forward and back again to focus on the snap and zipper of Juandre's cargo pants. "I'm going to undress you, and then I'm going to fuck you right here against the wall, Daddy," I said, sounding feral and hungry. "I'm in charge tonight. Your sneaky ass needs punishment."

"Yes, please," Juandre uttered, accentuating the esses in my ear. I flung him around and switched places so his chest pressed against the spot my back just heated.

"Palms flat against the wall. Don't move," I commanded, and Juandre followed my orders obediently. I fell to my knees behind him and removed his shoes and pants. "Spread your legs, Daddy," I said, enjoying watching him eagerly open them for me. I left his shirt on since it was cold against the black marble tiles.

I grabbed Juandre's muscled glutes, squashing and squeezing them softly and pulling them wide, exposing and softening his hole.

"Good god, boy!" Juandre exclaimed as I bit into his left butt cheek. I wanted to sink my fangs into them, but this wasn't the time. Juandre's masculine musk aroused the fuck out of me, so I reached around Juandre's hip and gave his cock a few hard tugs.

"Ah yes, just like that," Juandre said approvingly, but I let go of his cock out of spite. My own was also painfully hard, protruding, and hanging out of the thin material of my Speedo bathing suit, which could not accommodate its size and weight. I pushed the sides down my hips, fully freeing my genitals from their confinement.

I stroked Juandre's hairy thighs, noticing that he tried his best to hold still for me, but he couldn't control the involuntary fine tremors in his upper legs. "Look how hungry you are for your boy to fuck you. Daddy, you're bloody quivering for me," I told him.

"Yes, boy, I fucking am. Please, do something, or I'll come all over this wall anyway."

"No, that won't do. It sounds to me like you need a cock ring. You want me to roll one on for you, Daddy?" I asked with a lustful voice in his ear.

"Yes, please. Please, Andrew, my boy," Juandre begged. Lucky for him, I had some supplies in my locker.

"Stand still, and don't move," I said and sprinted to my locker, grabbing a bottle of lube and cock ring.

"I'm back," I said, putting him at ease. He must have felt the movement of wind on his ass, but he didn't say a word. I guessed he expected that, since he thought I was a vampire.

"Come here," I said while pulling him back to me. I reached around him, applying a bit of lube, squeezing and pulling the skin tight over his cock. Then I rolled the ring down to the base. Juandre hissed and swore. I tested the movement of the silky skin covering my Daddy's penis with hard downward and lighter upward strokes.

"Andrew, I don't think... your plan... is working, my boy. Ugh." Juandre groaned in ecstasy.

He's coming.

I grasped my leaking cock, smearing the residual lube over it, and then pushed it against his tight hole and forced my cock head into his sphincter.

"Oh, my fucking god!" Juandre screamed. The words reverberated over the swimming pool water and into the night. I held onto his hips, pushing deeper and savoring the tight pressure and heat of his hole.

Despite the pain, he'd not pulled away. Instead, he begged for more. "Fuck me, boy, Andrew, please, Andrew, I need this."

I have dreamed of this.

"Oh, fuck!" he repeated.

I didn't reply but answered Juandre's plea by pushing the remaining length of my cock deep into him. We stood there, not moving, flushed together —both quivering. I panted, and Juandre gasped between crying, whimpers, and begging for more. I waited until I felt Juandre relaxing, then pulled out and slammed back into him.

"You feel so fucking good!" I roared as I pulled out and pushed back again. "I doubt I can go any longer," I said and held still on the precipice of an orgasm.

"Hammer me, Andrew," Juandre begged, even as he stilled.

"I missed you for so long. I thought our love-making would at least be longer than five minutes," I said, licking and savoring the sweat off Juandre's shoulder. I had him tagged, yet Juandre still hadn't moved. Just for that alone, I knew I loved him already.

"May I bite your shoulder? I want to taste your blood on my tongue when I come deep inside you."

"Will you turn me into a vampire?" Juandre asked, panting.

I chuckled, "No, I'm not a vampire. I'm only breaking your skin, only a scratch for one drop of your blood." I could taste his blood already, but I waited for Juandre's consent.

"Yes... you may," he finally said, and I groaned as I used my right fang, like a needle, and pierced his skin.

Tiny prickles, like minute electric sparkles, danced through my body, and I moaned deep guttural sounds of delight as Juandre's blood flowed over my tongue. "I'm coming!" My voice was guttural and low, droning like a giant waking up after eons of sleeping under mountains. My body contracted and convulsed, my knees wanted to buckle, and I hung onto Juandre.

"I'm not stopping. I want more." Juandre grunted, and the quick sloshing sounds told me Juandre was pummeling his own cock. I reached around to grab hold of Juandre's heavy ball sack. I left my cock where it was, inside Juandre's ass and still tapping his prostate.

"I'm going to cum!" Juandre said hurriedly.

"Yes, you are, you beautiful, handsome man," I whispered into his ear, taking another lick of blood from the trapezius muscle over his scapula. Then, I pulled my cock out and ordered, "Turn around, come in my mouth, Daddy."

Juandre turned instantly, and I fell to my knees. With a quick grab, pull, roll, I slipped my Daddy's cock ring off. Juandre weaved his fingers through my hair and pushed his cock deep into my mouth, forcefully, as I retracted my fangs and swallowed him down my throat.

"Ahh fuck!" Juandre hissed out, pulling my face into the nest of his trimmed pubic hair. "Don't stop sucking. Don't stop... oh, my boy, fuck, please don't stop! It feels so damned fucking good! Oh, god, boy, never have... ever!" Juandre yelled as he blasted his cum down my throat.

I swallowed and swallowed, not allowing a drop to escape my mouth. I wanted all of my Daddy's cum inside me. He tasted exquisite, and I knew I would never let him go again.

"Hello! It's Randy, Juandre's friend. The business meeting you had... is it over? Are you two done? I want to go home." Juandre's friend called from outside the pool area. I was still on my feet and tucking our still half-hard cocks back into underwear and speedos. Then I helped Juandre get his cargo pants up then quickly wrapped a towel around my waist.

"Where to now?" I asked a chuckling Juandre.

"Where are you?" Randy yelled. "We're looking for you. Juandre and Andrew? I have two guards with me," Randy sing-songed as he called. He was smart. As gay men, we knew anyone could be a bigot, and out of mutual concern, we stuck together. *Their footsteps were getting closer.*

Laughing, Juandre and I scrambled and fell on the pool deck chairs, pretending we had been talking. Then Randy and two human guards appeared.

"Ah, there you are, sir. We found this one

hanging around and wanted to make sure he's with you, sir," the bigger of the two guards said in a southern drawl.

"Yes, everything's fine. They came by tonight instead of tomorrow, and we have just wrapped it up," I said and waited.

No one spoke. The smell of semen drifted with the chlorinated mist. I hoped it was only me smelling it and that the sharp chlorine was masking it. My security guards seemed uncomfortable and perplexed.

"I'll call it in and clear the alert. Sorry for disturbing you, sir." The big guy nodded, and the other guard stepped forward.

"So sorry, sir," the other guard said with interest. He wasn't looking sorry when he noticed Juandre sprawled on the chair beside me.

"Nothing to be sorry about. You were only doing your job, so thank you," I replied as I noticed the unapologetic, intentional eagerness to see Juandre's face.

"Do you need anything, sir?" he asked, not taking his gaze off Juandre, which I didn't appreciate. Juandre offered a weak wave to him as if to say "hello." I disliked that even more, as I wanted to keep Juandre all to myself and hold onto him.

"No, thank you, my man. Good night. You may be on your way." I excused them shortly. I didn't know these men, but I was sure they were Disciples. I would have to ask Tony tomorrow who they were. I brushed their inquisitiveness off as they probably couldn't believe Juandre and Randy had snuck by them. I hoped that was the reason as they turned to leave.

When they were out of earshot, Randy whispered, "Buggering much? It sounded like you were mauling each other in here." He pointed to the open-plan gym and pool area around us. "It's empty and hollow. Sound travels far at night. They probably heard the two of you all the way to the main road."

"How did the two of you sneak by them?" I wanted to know.

"I don't know, we just drove in and parked the car. They didn't stop us," Randy said, and I pointed to a chair, indicating he should sit down.

"I'm thirsty. Anyone in the mood for whiskey?" I asked, smiling at Juandre, who flapped a wrist lazily.

CHAPTER 6
JUANDRE

CREEPY GREGORIAN CHANTING WOKE ME. *WE MUST BE underground. It's humid, cold, and musty.* My thoughts rushed, trying to make sense of where I was. I thought I was in Rome for a moment, hearing the Latin plainsong I had grown up with. Men in black robes chanted the medieval musical notes on their knees, surrounding me. On my right side was an altar adorned with all kinds of relics and papyrus rolls. On my left was a small table and one chair. High on the wall behind them, tapestries hung. *It must be an underground church.* Embroidery of a white dove sat on a robed figure's shoulder as the man pointed his hands up to the sky, to the moon. A gigantic hand reached down, fingers open as if reaching to pick the figure up.

I watched the leader, puzzled and afraid for my life. He wore a black robe with golden lapels on the back of his neck and draped over his shoulders. He'd been chanting Latin and speaking English with a Middle Eastern accent. As he continued, the men repeated what he said, sounding like a mindless cult.

Am I an offering? What do they want from me? I searched for clues. My gaze fell on that table to my right again. I squinted to see through the hazy fog. They drugged me with something. Shaking my head to clear the cobwebs and sober up, I noticed upon clearer inspection of the apparatus. *Torture devices!*

They looked ancient and rusted and designed to inflict maximum pain. I was panic-stricken. If they used any of those on me, and I didn't die of blood loss, I was definitely checking out with tetanus—spastic and never-ending seizures. The sight of them horrified me, and I screamed. A piece of cloth was then shoved in my mouth—so lots of hmmm-hmmm sounds and no words were emitted, but it didn't stop me from yelling.

The horrid chanting continued. Either they couldn't hear me, or they ignored me. A helmet with a lock, a weird corkscrew hand drilling thing for bones, pliers, and hammers had been laid out on the farthest end of the table. I strained my neck to see the rest of it... *Oh, and fifteen-centimeter nails. Also rusted.*

Sweat beaded on my hairline and ran in rivulets down my temples. My groin itched and burned. It was damp and reeked of urine. *It must have happened when I was unconscious.* My eyes weren't covered. That was a bad sign. Around my head, they tied a cloth that kept the ball of material inside my mouth. They restrained me by tying my hands behind my back and my feet to the legs of a chair.

I couldn't remember how I got into this situation. The last thing I remembered was climbing into bed, wanking, and falling asleep.

They must have broken into my house and abducted me without waking me up. They drugged me. My head feels woozy, like the time I'd taken that Extasy pill with Randy. No, that was the time I took the shrooms. Stop it, focus, Juandre. Yes, focus, even if everywhere I look is fuzzy.

I recognized the *Dies Irae*, a chant from the 13th century and possibly earlier. The title refers to the "Day of Wrath."

"Dies irae, dies illa

Solvet saeclum in favilla

Teste David cum Sibylla

Quantus tremor est futurus

Quando Judex est venturus

Cuncta stricte discussurus!

I TRANSLATED IT INTO ENGLISH.

Will break up the world into ash

As testified by David and the Sybil

The day of wrath, the day of wrath, that day

Will break up the world into ash

The day of wrath, that day

Will break up the world into ash

As testified by David and the Sybil.

The day of wrath, the day of wrath, that day

Will break up the world into ash

THE LEADER STEPPED FORWARD and spoke. The others got up from their knees.

"My assumptions about the conflict in our organization will soon be clear to us. I have concluded that the next step to defer the chaos is crucial. We have waited a long time," he announced, and the others hummed in agreement.

He lifted his arms and spoke. "We achieved success by working hard, not just relying on our leaders," he boomed, his voice echoing in the cavernous hall. They hummed again.

Damn this, I decided. I needed to get out of what looked like an underground temple. I wiggled my wrists, looking for something sharp to cut the ties. I saw nothing.

The leader continued. "That which was preserved for us is why we are certain and wholly devout today. I assumed our leaders could lead us to create communities that would save us and let us live with our divine gods." He paused and looked over the crowd, then at me. I stopped fidgeting with the loose ties.

Keep talking. As long as you're talking, you're not cutting me up. I searched for escape routes. *Once free, I'm running and getting out of this place.* They'd forced the cloth deep into my mouth, and it was setting off my gag reflex. I hung my head low, forcing the vomit through my nasal cavity. Knowing I was on the verge of aspirating on my vomit and fearful of drowning, I strained to breathe through my nose.

Andrew went home, back to his office. His board

of directors had called an urgent meeting. *Please notice I'm gone. Please find me.* Andrew said Tony could find anyone anywhere. *And if I died, would he ever find my body? Would he bury and mourn me? What will happen to Charlie?*

I hoped Charlie was okay. He was at his mother's. Thank the fates for that.

"Our promise will be fulfilled when our communities come together. To live and walk among our true creators and divine beings. It will be a time of no trouble, and I promise you, our time of waiting has ended. We will live exalted because we were the ones who carried the flame, the message to the chosen of humankind. We are a handful of scholars, but we are the chosen and gifted Disciples of the Anunnaki!" he roared, and they clapped their hands. Their robes sounded like linen rattling in the wind.

They're all crazy. What are the Anunnaki?

"Yes, rejoice, scholars, for we are the people who nourish the future for life as everlasting as it should be."

"As it should be," they repeated like it was their mantra.

I was in deep shit. At least my hands were loose now. I'd twisted and abraded the skin on my wrists, so the blood acted as lubrication to slip my hands out of their confinements. I kept them in place behind my back, hiding them.

"Our purpose is practical, academic, intelligent, careful, intensive but straightforward, not to obscure and hide but operate under their watch."

"To operate under their watch," his audience chanted.

Oh, god, the leader's coming my way!

"Juandre," he called my name as if he knew me.

I couldn't see his face, the hood of his cloak darkened it.

My feet are still tied. I couldn't run. Tears streamed down my face, and I shook my head from side to side. The leader stepped closer.

"Juandre, do you see these?" He pointed to the altar, which looked like a museum exhibition. "I translated and paraphrased these. They're scriptural passages written thousands of years ago. You are fortunate. Do you know why?"

I shook my head, my ears zinged, and it felt like I was going to pass out. I gulped for oxygen through my nose and then heaved again, desperately trying not to inhale the vomit. I was about to remove the gag, but the man beat me to it with one tug.

I gasped and coughed and vomited again. I was a mess, but managed to keep my loosened hands hidden. When I somewhat collected myself, I lifted my head and searched for a face I could identify later.

"I asked you a question. Do you know how lucky you are, Juandre?" he asked with a sickly smile.

His voice was pompously high, like a female voice, but not. As he spoke, he held his head high and stiffly spoke down his nose. It was as if he thought he was royalty and I was a measly peasant. I wouldn't be surprised if they were all castrated. The robes, the chanting, and the aloof, high-pitched voices convinced me they were monks.

Yeah, come to think of it, they all sound a bit lacking in the testosterone department. Oh, my god, is that what the table with tools is for? Are they planning to cut my genitals off?

The man kicked at the foot of my chair. "Answer me!"

"No!" I shouted on a wheeze. The hooded men in the background chuckled.

He walked over to the table, pointing to a flat big rock. "These tablets say how important you are. Your son will lead men and will take us all to the moon. Your son will be a Disciple." He walked back over to me. A righteous aura of menace radiated off him.

Take us to the moon? Has he lost it? My Charlie is only ten years old.

"Your father has connections in Rome. You know that, don't you? We have been searching for you. It wasn't until your divorce and your wife changed your son's last name to her last name, Montgomery, that we found you. We have Rome's authorization to teach you good morals, which your father and ex-wife approved. Sign these papers and leave Charlie with his mother."

"What are you talking about? I never permitted her to change my Charlie's name. And what does my father have to do with this? I haven't seen him in years," I asked, looking at the papers on a small table.

The hooded men in the peanut gallery chuckled again.

"You obviously don't know how to pleasure a woman, so I guess your father stepped in to help you."

Now, it all made sense. I had never slept with Chrissy. The paternity tests were incorrect, after all. The nucleotide markers could have suggested it was me, but they could also point to my father.

"Are you saying Charlie isn't even my son? He's my half-brother! But I love him. I raised him." My heart broke—*all the deceit.* "Where are they? I want to talk to them," I demanded, spittle flying.

"They are waiting for you to decide. Vanish from Charlie's life on your terms, or we indoctrinate you until you forget your perverted ways."

"What? So you want to castrate me? Cut off my balls, and you think being gay will disappear? Do you hear yourselves? You all sound like a bunch of schoolgirls! Are you even aware your gonads excrete that testosterone? Cutting off someone's balls doesn't make him more male, you dumb prick!"

"My name is Gordon Fincher," the leader said, removing his hood. He was okay in the looks department, but his evil intent made him terrifyingly ugly as a demon from the lowest level of hell.

"Perhaps you will be more accommodating to your family if you understand who's in charge here." He pointed to the others, who still hadn't removed their hoods. "Your father sends his regards because no father wants to see his son cleansed. After today, I believe you'll abandon your immoral lifestyle and raise Charlie with a backbone, laying a solid foundation for him and his new brothers."

"We haven't spoken to each other in years. I don't need his regards! And I don't care about my ex-wife!" I yelled. My father was a rich asshole who cared more about what his friends would say than his son's happiness. And it seemed my ex-wife had my father's cock in hand. "Thank you. You just confirmed what I suspected all these years. They're two heads of one monster."

"Tsk-tsk," Gordon spat at me. I shook my head, trying to rid it of the foul spittle.

I wanted to go home and face the two who had forced me into that fake marriage. I had made a life for myself, even though I needed my father's money to finish my education. But for all the years after, I had needed him more than his money. My father had left me and my mother all alone while he traveled the world, most probably with Chrissy.

My stomach was churning. My worst fears were unfolding. I knew this wasn't good for me, especially if my father and ex-wife were involved.

"Please, Gordon. I have no clue what you're talking about and what my father and ex-wife have done. Are you the mafia or something? Do I have to pay for the sins of my father? Just please let me go, or let's contact my father so I can find out what's going on. Does he owe you money? Why are you taking my son?" I asked, desperately trying to make sense of this.

"No, not just mafia, but you're on the correct

path. We have those traits. We comprise many of those groups. For example, I am LAZ. That's a Caucasian ethnic group originally from the Middle East. But we influence many regions and many religions in that area. We are from many parts of the world. Your father and I are good friends. We all consider you a friend, too. After all, you're Charles's father. All of us here want to be your friend."

If I see my father again, I'm going to strangle him. What had he gotten himself, me, into?

Gordon turned to his men. "What do you think, men? Shall we start with his cleansing?"

"It's getting late," a hooded man said, and Gordon looked at him with an evil grin.

What are these crazy sons of bitches up to? I wished I knew. My answer came as if they heard me asking.

They were all shedding their robes and standing naked in front of me. Unsmiling, their lifeless eyes focused on me. They seemed to be of different ages. The youngest looked about twenty-five, and I guessed Gordon was the oldest, about my father's age, if not older. Some seemed castrated, and others did not. Fear, as I had never felt before, assailed me. I heaved breaths of air as my heartbeat sped up at the sight of their mutilated bodies.

"What are you doing? What do you want with me?" I asked no one in particular.

"You will know soon enough. We've arranged a special time for you," Gordon told me with a sickening smile.

"Show him, turn him around, and untie him," Gordon ordered the youngest. He jumped to get something from their apparatus table, probably a knife, and that was when I took my chance. I reached up and grabbed Gordon's engorged prick, and with all the strength I could muster, I twisted. As a trauma surgeon, I knew precisely how to rupture the tunica albuginea. I heard a crackling, then a popping sound, and I knew I was successful when Gordon screamed.

Right before a fist connected with my jaw, I held on and twisted it in the opposite direction for good measure. My chair and I fell to the side, skidding over the dirty tiled floor.

Gordon howled, and someone screamed, "No, don't touch it. We must take him to the hospital!"

Another one said, "What will we tell them happened?"

I couldn't focus. Everything was dull, and things swam in my field of vision. I had a concussion. The noise of men yelling sounded like I was underwater.

I shook my head. Salty blood and spittle ran from my nose and mouth.

I heard someone volunteer to take him to the emergency room. "I'll cover him in his robe. He won't be able to put pants on anyway."

I let my head fall to the ground and closed my eyes as I prayed for Tony and Andrew to find me. My feet were still tied, but my hands were free, and I remembered.

Opening my eyes, I scanned the surroundings.

It's time to run.

I slipped my feet from their confinements.

"Oh shit! Fuck no!" I yelled as two of them grabbed me, hauled me into the air, and carried me to the back of the cavern. One struggled with my belt, but was too slow. The other man ripped my pants and pulled them down, then took off my underwear.

"You pissed yourself." They laughed.

"Put him in the swing and tie him up. I don't want to get hurt like Gordon," a deep voice to my left said.

"Stop!" Gordon ordered.

What? Gordon? Did he come back? Perhaps I never fractured his cock. Did he want to go first? My thoughts spun, trying to make sense of the chaos.

"He said stop," a voice similar to Andrew's said.

Then, like a flock of birds, they scattered as the sounds of a roaring madman spun around me and echoed off the walls. Howls of pain and gasps accompanied the unmistakable cracking of bones, dull thuds, and tearing flesh.

I saw a blur of motion. Men running and flying. I struggled to see what was happening. I was sure Andrew had come for me, and he was on a rampage. Only he could move like the wind. Screaming and begging filled the cavern just like I had just done.

Snapping, cracking, breaking, gurgling, and ferocious growls and hisses like a wildcat.

I turned my head this and that way to see behind me and noticed Tony's friendly face. Tony covered my body with a robe and wrapped me inside it. It was a bloodbath around us. It seemed Andrew had broken their necks and ripped all their arms off. Naked male bodies, their heads at unnatural angles, were strewn like confetti.

I whimpered, and my cries filled the sudden silence. Then Andrew stood in front of me.

"Dammit, I was too late. I'm so sorry, baby," he said repeatedly while rubbing and checking for broken bones. "Sick Disciple bastards!" Andrew's deep baritone echoed over the stench of death. He was drenched in blood—even his face. He'd used his teeth. *Most probably.*

"No, you came just in time. T—thank you, thank you," I said through chattering teeth and sank towards the ground, relieved and exhausted.

"My love!" Andrew caught me in midair. Strong arms enveloped me. "I'm taking you away from this place," he said, carrying me like I weighed nothing.

"Before you go, sir," Tony said. "Should I bring the relics?"

"Yes, please. Only bring the tablets and scrolls." Andrew sounded livid. I could hear it in his voice. This comforted me, as I finally felt protected.

"Tony, can you get someone in to clean up my mess and get rid of those bodies? Torch it all. That will also get rid of those damn torture devices. We knew this day was coming. Follow the plan. Thanks. I'm taking him to the hospital," he said over his shoulder.

"Don't worry, baby, I'll take all this away and make you forget them. Do you want to remember or forget? It's your choice, whatever you need," Andrew asked as we exited the building.

The last yellow rays of the sun blinded me as it sank behind the mountainous tree line. "I was gone for a whole day," I blubbered.

It sounded like Andrew was crying. "I'm taking you to the hospital. Hold on. I'm so very sorry, my love," Andrew said, voice cracking.

"No, take me home. I'm okay. I don't want to go to the hospital. Everyone will recognize me." I objected in a moment of fearful clarity. And shame. My strength was draining. "I just want a bath and a bed. And then I want to forget this day."

"What about testing and anti-virals? Are you— aren't you hurt?" Andrew asked, scooping me into his blue *BMW* and buckling my seatbelt. As we drove off, I noticed they had held me in a secluded stone building.

"No, you came just in time, just before..."

"Thank the fates!"

"You're full of blood. You can't go to the ER like that, Andrew. I want to lie in your arms, and you can help me forget this when I fall asleep tonight. Can you do that for me?" I asked sleepily. The adrenalin was wearing off.

"Of course, I can, and I will," Andrew answered, stroking up and down my leg while he drove us away.

"They knew me. My Charlie, my father, and Chrissy," I said between sobs. "It was so confusing. They said Charlie isn't mine. He's my father and

Chrissy's," I cried. "Can you find out what's going on and why, Andrew? Do you think Tony can go get Charlie and keep him safe?"

"Yes, I will. We have the relics now. I will fix this —just rest. Close your eyes. You can sleep a bit."

"Thank you for saving me. I must remember to thank Tony." I mumbled. "How did you know where to find me?" I asked groggily without opening my eyes.

"Tony. He had a tracker on your car. It seems they packed a bag, took your phone, and wanted to make it look like you were going somewhere. I started looking for you when I smelled them in the house. Otherwise, I would have thought you left."

"What? My car and phone were here? Weird. Do you think they wanted to kill me? Did my father and Chrissy ask for this? I knew they hated me, but this was extreme."

"Don't know. Tony and I will sort this out. You're safe now. Gordon was the leader of the American Disciples. This was their compound. I'll explain later when you can listen better. Tomorrow, okay? They can't hurt you anymore. Not you or Charlie."

"Hmmm." I believed Andrew and drifted off into a peaceful sleep.

CHAPTER 7
ANDREW

Gripping my Nokia so tightly that the plastic creaked under the strain, I answered Tony. "Yes, he's asleep now. Did you take care of things like I asked?"

"Yes, sir!" Tony said over the phone. I relaxed and loosened my grip on the cell phone and turned to watch Juandre sleep. His breathing was slow and deep, and his permanent smile was back, even in sleep. I pulled the duvet over his shoulder, making sure he was covered and warm.

Tony continued speaking. "We torched the place. There is nothing left of the American chapter, sir."

"And Charlie?"

"Our contacts had just confirmed that Chrissy and Juandre's mother and father had just arrived at their villa in Marsala. I'm on my way to retrieve him. I had to wake the captain and ask him to prepare the jet. It's being fueled and waiting at the company hangar. I figured since no one on your board of directors would mind me using it." He chuckled cynically. "I'm taking five men; they are waiting to meet me on the tarmac."

"Italy?"

"Yes."

"Good, don't let Charlie see, but you know what you have to do," I whispered, making my way to the living room to start closing all the curtains in the house. "I'm staying here with Juandre until I know he is okay. Once Charlie is back, I'm planning to take them to South Africa."

"Don't worry, sir. I have five of our best men with me."

"I'm not worried. I don't know what I would have done without my team." My voice was loaded with the stress and worry of the day. But I kept my emotions threatening to break my resolve at bay. I caught my naked reflection in the window. I was pale, and dark circles swallowed my eyes. I thought I would need a feeding soon, and I closed the blinds before I pulled the curtains covering them. "Oh, and Tony," I said.

"Yes, sir."

"Thank you for helping me find Juandre just in time today. Good job."

"No problem, I'm here to help you. As long as you share a few drops of your blood with me now and then." His optimism always made me smile. Tony loved being my Igigi. Something I learned from Ishtar during his many visits searching for his mate after we chased my first Igigi, Elijah, onto his time machine, but we were too slow to catch him. Now, that was a long story for another day, I thought. I had so much to share with Juandre.

"We just passed security. I see the men getting out of the Hummer. Okay, we're going to be boarding the jet. I will bring Charlie to you once we're back on US soil," Tony said. I heard the rumble of the jet engines starting up.

"We're going to have to go dark for a while. I don't have a board of directors left. I'm sure the police would come sniffing."

"I know. I have a backup plan for our backup plan."

"You are the best. Thanks, Tony."

"Did you scrub Juandre's memory? Did he ask you to?"

"I did, but I'm unsure if I even did it correctly."

"You will see tomorrow. I have to go. We're taking off. Have to switch off now."

"Sure. Bye."

I placed the phone on the bedside table and got into bed with Juandre. I snuggled closer behind him. He mumbled something but went right back to sleep.

This was the most eventful day of my life. I've never killed someone with my bare hands and teeth, but today, I just proved that I'm a monster. I love Juandre more than anything else. I'm sure he is my mate. Judging by the animalistic possessiveness that came over me when I entered that stone building, when I heard Juandre's screams.

I told him I would take care of everything and deal with everyone who hurt him or Charlie.

My heart broke when he said, "Many people have been through worse. I am ashamed and so stupid. So belittled. He was trembling in my arms as I bathed him. As he fell asleep, I entered his mind and erased the past day as best I could.

Tears streamed down my face. "I love you," I said, sobbing soundlessly until I fell asleep.

CHAPTER 8
JUANDRE

I JOLTED AWAKE TO ANDREW GRUNTING AND SEEMINGLY having a nightmare. Worried, I woke him as gently as I could. Andrew was ice cold. Switching on the bedside lamp, I saw his pale, sweaty face. This must have been a terrible nightmare, I thought as I saw his wide, bewildered eyes pop open, the leftover adrenaline still in his system.

"Holy shit, Andrew, are you okay? Look at me! You are safe," I said, patting his cheeks and wiping the tiny beads of sweat from his forehead to help him refocus on the here and now.

His breathing slowed, and his big round pupils shrank, revealing the green irises as his stare met mine. When he'd calmed down, I pulled Andrew out of my bedroom by the arm and into the kitchen, then sat him down at the kitchen island. I thought I'd gone to bed early the night before after suffering from a massive migraine since yesterday. I realized I'd slept for almost twenty-four hours when I checked my cell phone. My head throbbed in sync with my pulse, and I rubbed my eyes to ease the pressure behind them.

I went to the fridge, took out two glasses, and filled them with milk. Then, I placed both glasses in the microwave. We wordlessly watched them spin while warming up. The microwave pinged, and I grabbed both glasses, shutting the microwave door with my elbow as I handed one to Andrew. "Thank you," Andrew said, rubbing his face and looking extremely troubled.

"Tell me, as a vampire, are you alive or dead now?" I asked as I pulled a chair out for myself and sat. It was four o'clock in the afternoon, but all the curtains were drawn to keep the sunlight outside. "I'd made up my mind. I want you to turn me into a vampire, but first, I need to know more about this. I don't want to say you should have told me this before, and then hate you. Tell me your honest story. How did you end up here today? Why do you have these nightmares? Is it because you drift between planes, and your soul can't rest? You're neither living nor dead. I heard you mumble something about being alive and dying, and you seemed to cry and fight with someone?"

Andrew chuckled cynically. "I'm glad you decided. I kind of already knew. As for killing people, I really can't answer that because I don't know what the dream was about. Lately, I've wanted to kill many people. I suppose it could be suppressed anger issues. As for being a vampire, I know it's not what you've read in books or seen on television. The word vampire is a made-up name from books. The person who gave me this gift had fangs, but he wasn't a vampire. He was something else.

"My memory has been diluted by the passing years, and although I remember significant things like smiles and laughter, the hows and whys that took place before are getting convoluted as the years pass. That's why I have nightmares. They come to refresh my mind. For example, think about a beautiful full moon that you've seen. And then try to remember what you were doing that specific night. You can't because the full moon impacted you, so your brain deletes useless information to make space for more."

"Oh yes, that's true," I said, thinking about

Charlie's birthday and not recalling what he wore that day. I smiled at Andrew with affection. We had always understood each other since our first meeting.

"Anyway, I would be an empty husk with a tortured mind if I had to recollect the scope of it all daily. I'll tell you the full story, and then I'll shelve it back under *open only in case of an emergency*, okay?"

"Maybe don't tell me if it will bother you like that," I said and meant it. I didn't want to ask anything if it meant hurting Andrew.

"No, I have to tell you, we're planning to be together, so I have to tell you. Sooner or later, I'll tell you about my friends and me. The things I've seen and the future I imagine coming to fruition sometimes scare me, and I need to share this with you, or my head will burst. They're memories of someone else, given to me to remind me of future things." Andrew seemed tired, like the fate of humanity rested on his shoulders. Those eyes that once sparkled so intensely now held emptiness as I sought what Andrew saw in his mind.

"Surely, Juandre... I'm not dead. I've been given a choice like I gave you one, but I was also born a certain way. Something was forced into me as a fetus and into my mother. I was an experiment. Luckily, my choices, which I'm currently working on, saved me from my family's clutches. I was made into this to enhance my ability to save others. And to save you."

CHAPTER 9
ANDREW

André, as relayed by Andrew to Juandre

1968 A.D.

West Berlin, Germany

It was early 1968 when I was forever changed. The protests against the Vietnam War had sparked widespread unrest, now referred to as the Nineteen Sixty-Eight generation. The call for liberation from our restrictive governments ignited both faculty and students. I celebrated with fellow protesters, having just earned my doctorate in chemical science and begun my tenured professorship.

I got swept up in the fray at the Opera House protests, then joined the celebrations of a triumphant march on solidarity and the abolition of national borders across Europe. It quickly turned into a night of loud music, dancing, and many shots of schnapps.

By midnight, I had to return to the apartment I shared with Peter, my best friend. He went home earlier, not liking crowds and preferring to finish packing. We had a train to catch at nine o'clock the following day that would take us to Vienna, then Switzerland, and, ultimately, we'd catch a flight to America.

Our fathers were professors of physics and science at the Humboldt University of Berlin. Still, the wall between East and West Berlin didn't prevent the organization from expanding into the West.

We had inherited our features. Peter, with his white-as-snow hair and crystal blue eyes, and I, with blond hair and green eyes, were from our fathers and had a unique bloodline bred from an ancient line of genetics. We were constantly measured and monitored, and being gay was punishable by death. Girls fell over their feet for us, but we were happy staying single as best friends.

We kept that a secret and insisted we were best friends and sometimes brothers because homosexuality was illegal. The organization known as the Disciples of the Anunnaki, responsible for the science and research faculty at Humboldt University, had offered each of us a position. We knew we had to seize the opportunity to escape their clutches and planned to do so the following morning. We faced disapproval if we associated with friends outside the organization. Even the apartment belonged to the university, which ultimately was owned by the organization. We intended to take our degrees and find work in America.

That night, I'd kept catching the eye of one oddly beautiful man. Each time our gazes locked, it was broken by some drunken patron passing between us.

Just before midnight, when my money was finished and I drank my fill of schnapps, I said my goodbyes and headed for the washroom to relieve myself before making the short walk home. It smelled dank and old, like all the beer halls in Vienna. I walked up to the long trough, which reeked of urine, pulled my cock out, and sighed in relief as a strong stream came out.

A deep male voice over my shoulder startled me. "*Very nice!*" I was shocked to see the handsome man I'd been ogling standing beside me, staring at my junk. The schnapps must have dulled my senses because I hadn't heard his entry or approach. I didn't respond but continued to empty myself into the enamel basin. I heard the sound of buttons unsnapping, and soon, his stream mingled with mine. I couldn't help but glance over to quickly see what he was up to packing.

He was standing much closer than was necessary. His dark cock was long and thick. I noticed he wore a golden ring of various sizes and designs on each of his long fingers because I watched intently as he relieved himself. He continually pulled his foreskin, retracting it and then pushing it forward over the large head. He never took his gaze off me. I was uncomfortable as fuck. Men did things like that to test you, and you ended up being battered to death in the alley. I stopped pissing and hastily tucked myself away to get out of there.

He purred at me, and his tone was minacious, accentuating the dark aura that emanated from him. "Why do you act so nervous? I'm sure there have been many men who compliment, perhaps even worship, such a fine cock as yours. It is made even more impressive by the body to which it is attached."

He was gorgeous, and everything about him screamed danger. Like a predator. A giant predator. I estimated him to be an easy eight feet tall. His lips were full, and his skin was smooth and hairless. His dark complexion didn't match his weird, golden eyes. His deep baritone alone had my cock taking notice.

I lied and said, "I'm not nervous." Even though I was already seeing him pounding into me relentlessly. And I wasn't sure if he wanted to fuck or kill me. "I've just stayed out later than I planned, and I have much to do," I answered shakily and turned to leave.

Before I reached the door, I felt a hand on my shoulder, which turned into a grip. I was turned around, and my back was shoved into the wall. He brought his face to mine and forced me into a rough kiss. I pushed him back and tried going for the door. Once again, he grabbed me and slammed me against the wall.

He leered at me. "Why are you in such a hurry? I only want to have a little fun," he hissed at me with a wanton look on his dark, angelically beautiful face. His voice was deeper than before. He must have been a fallen angel because he emanated immoral and shameless debauchery.

I begged, "Please, I just want to go home." I'd never been so frightened or sexually aroused.

Still holding me against the wall, he demanded, "What is your name, boy?"

I was no boy. I was in my thirties. He was getting some delight from seeing the fear in my eyes.

"An... André," I stuttered.

He nodded slowly. "André," he said. Then he took a shiny electronic device from his pocket and held it beside my face. I wondered what it was and why he asked my name. I was worried our fathers sent him to collect us.

He put the device back in his pocket. "That is a very German name. You should change it when you reach America. You're going to be very famous one day," he said slowly.

Fuck, he knew about our plans. My cock deflated instantly as my system flooded with adrenaline, and I wished someone would enter the restroom so that I could flee. I focused on his eyes in the light, which had a sheen to them, like an animal. His irises were something I'd never seen before. They had rings of gold and black around the pupils.

I wasn't going to let him know how scared I was that he was right. "I'm a professor at West Berlin University. I'm not going to America. You must have me confused with someone else," I said, mesmerized by his otherworldly eyes and hoping to reason with him.

He continued looking at my face as if he'd memorized it and confirmed I was who he thought I was. "You are from my lover's city. It is a pity we did not travel to meet each other earlier. So we have to work with the time we have. Don't worry. We will have enough time to have a good time." He seemed to ooze out the last three words, then smiled, revealing pointy white incisor teeth.

Still hoping to convince him to let me go, I asked, "I don't understand what you mean. Why would you have a lover and still want me? Won't he be jealous? I would be jealous. I really need to get on my way."

"But of course you do," he said as he tilted his head from side to side, his gaze never leaving me, lingering on my lips. I licked them involuntarily. My cock was back to being achingly hard, and the big man overpowering me turned me on. I was not small when compared to Peter, but in this man's presence, I was the itty-bitty mouse, and he was the lion.

"Yes, please," I said, not knowing why or what I agreed to. I didn't even know where our conversation was leading, but I was sure it was not to a virtuous place.

He smiled at me and, with a serious look, said, "André, I am Ishtar, but you can call me Ish. I'm looking for a group that calls themselves the Disciples. You have heard of them, yes?" he asked and hissed through his lengthening incisors.

"How could I not have heard of them?" I stupidly answered truthfully. I took the opportunity to slide toward the door to get out of his reach because Peter and I came from prominent families that primarily belonged to the stupid psychotic group. "I wish you a good night," I told him.

I mustered a smile and turned to the door when I heard his deep, authoritative voice. "I did not give you permission to leave."

My breath hitched. "I apologize. I thought our conversation was over. I didn't mean to be rude," I said calmly. Inside, I felt lightheaded and was on the verge of panicking.

"André, I forgive you, but you must make it up to me," he responded. It sounded like a lisp as he spoke through the teeth hanging out the sides of his mouth. "Don't be scared," he said.

My fight-or-flight response betrayed me. I wanted to run or fall down and play dead, but instead, I stood shaking and it wasn't from fear. I was excited by the hunger in his eyes for me. I let my gaze fall on his impressive bulge.

"How... what do you mean? What do you plan to do to me?" I asked, not wanting to know, yet eager for an answer.

"Go through the door at the end of the hall. That will take you into an alley. I will be right behind you. Do not even think of running," he said as a purr. "I will catch you."

He gestured for me to leave, and I obeyed. I was scared his buddies were waiting, ready to bash my head in for being attracted to men. I had no choice, so I pushed the heavy door at the end of the hall open and walked out into the crisp night air.

The alley was completely empty except for cans of trash. A full moon peeked through the opening between the two buildings. The sounds of people, cars, and horns curtained us from the world outside, so close, but still out of my reach. When I turned around, Ish leaned against the brick wall of the building we'd just exited. He stared at me, looking deep into my soul. A look only one man can give another, a look of lust and hunger that only a man could satisfy. A woman would cower under that gaze, and I was no woman.

"Don't be afraid, tell me now, do you want this or not?" he asked soothingly as he unbuttoned his green and gold crisp uniform coat. It looked aristocratic from another era. "I just want you to do what you so obviously enjoy doing with that pretty mouth."

"I don't know what you mean," I responded, knowing my lies were falling on deaf ears. And I liked it.

The smile left his face. "Over here in front of me now and on your knees, boy," he ordered me. I could see that he was serious and meant every word. I should have taken the opportunity to say no and run. But my body betrayed me. My cock stirred at his command, and I knew I liked it. I walked up to him and sank to my knees.

"There now, be a good boy and take out my cock." Once again, he was speaking in his catlike purr with no signs of anger, only authoritative dominance. I wanted to keep him purring, so I reached out and undid his belt buckle and methodically began unclasping the weird hooks of his pants' front.

"Ah, there's a good boy. Now reach in and pull it out."

Gingerly, I put my fingers through the opening

of his underwear. I was surprised to find no hair at all. It was silky smooth. I caught the scent of male musk and felt the root of his cock, which was thickening even as I grasped it and pulled it into the open air, where it continued to respond to my eager manipulation. He was huge, and I shivered as I enjoyed doing what I was ordered.

"Put it in your mouth and suckle it, boy. Suck on my piss slit," he said through his abnormally long incisors.

I did as I was told. I opened my mouth wide and tried to cover my teeth with my lips. As his cock slid into my mouth, the thick foreskin was retracted from the sensitive head, and he gasped. I tasted the bitterness of unwashed cock and the sweetness of fluid leaking from his slit but didn't pull off. I swallowed eagerly.

"That's right, clean it. Wash it, pretty boy," he whispered and ran his hand through my hair, signaling his approval. I complied and hoped he wasn't working for the people we planned to run from in the morning. Maybe he was collecting intelligence against us. He knew about us and our plans.

Ish placed his hands behind my head and held me in place as he thrust into my mouth. Spit and pre-cum dripped out of my lips and down my chin.

His thrusts became fast and frantic, jabbing down my throat. The bulbous head of his cock intruded past my tonsils, and I couldn't breathe.

No man had ever had such a spell over me. Grunting and pulling my hair, he held my head firmly in place. He pulled back for a minute, just long enough for me to get a breath of fresh air, and in the back of my mind, I found quietness, silence, and peace. With the new air entering my lungs, full consciousness returned.

Ish prolonged the delicious sinful act of one man sucking another off by pulling out and staving off ejaculation. With my head still held in place, I rolled my eyes up to see his grinning face looking down at me.

I thought I heard the door open and shut, and then I saw another man beside Ish. Startled at being caught, I tried jumping up and away.

"No! Don't stop," Ish ordered, holding me in place by my hair. "This is my lover, Peter." He introduced us as if I wasn't holding his cock warm in my mouth. "I'm sure Peter will want to enjoy you when I have finished. Peter is also from here. Tonight is a reunion of some sort. Am I correct, Peter?"

Peter smiled and seemed delighted to see me like that. He was also dressed in a style of clothes I'd never seen in Berlin. He wasn't nearly as tall as Ish, who must be more than seven feet tall. His long hair was white-as-snow, and he almost looked exactly like my roommate, Peter. Even the blue eyes were the same. This Peter's hair cascaded over his shoulders. My Peter had short hair—otherwise, I would have said it was the same person.

"I think that he likes being on his knees. Is he good at this, Ish?" Peter appraised me up and down, lingering on my swollen lips.

"He is superb. It took a little convincing, but I can assure you that he's done this before," Ish said with an amused sparkle in his predatory eyes, then returned his attention to me. "Get going, boy. I don't have all night. The sooner you finish me off, the sooner you can suck Peter."

I resumed my sucking on his fat cock head in all earnest. Peter stood to our side and watched me fellating his lover. Ish was soon back into rhythm, pumping my mouth fiercely as he moaned and held my head in place. Tears were streaming from my eyes as he fucked my mouth.

"Peter, take your cock out and get it ready for our young friend," Ish ordered his lover.

Peter laughed and undid his pants. His staff, already erect, was long and thin with a wicked curve to it. As he watched me, he manipulated his foreskin slowly... almost casually. From the corner of my eye, I could see the glint of liquid oozing from the yawning tip.

"As always, Ish, you like a good mouth fucking," Peter approvingly said as he looked at us.

"Peter put your hand on my cock and feel it slide in and out of this boy's mouth and kiss me while he milks me." His voice was ragged with lustful urgency and without further hesitation, Peter placed a hand on Ish's shaft, where my lips would touch him whenever Ish's thick cock slammed into my throat.

At the same time, he bent his head toward Peter, who I noticed had regular human teeth. Ish became so excited by his lover's actions that I felt his balls rise against my chin. His cock swelled to an almost unbearable thickness as it shot thick wads of cum against the back of my throat.

I was on the border of losing consciousness from lack of oxygen when Ish pulled out of my throat and wiped what remained of his ejaculate against the side of my face.

No sooner had he withdrawn before he grabbed the length of Peter's staff and guided it to my mouth. Peter gasped, moaned, laced his fingers in my hair, and shoved himself into me, hard and deep. His cock, being slim, went down much further than Ish's and into the distinct curvature of my already bruised throat. I gagged and coughed and tried to pull back, which resulted in Peter pulling his cock out of my mouth. Peter and Ish both laughed.

"Now suck it right and don't pull back, or I won't be so nice next time! You're doing great. You're such a good boy," Peter praised, sounding precisely like my Peter. The lack of oxygen and euphoria intensified my enjoyment of being used, and I ejaculated in my pants.

Now Ish grabbed Peter's length and held on to it as my mouth was assailed. Peter didn't last as long as Ish. In just a matter of minutes came the familiar swell and release of sperm. Unlike his lover, Peter didn't force himself further down my throat as he orgasmed. Instead, he pulled out and, holding my head in place, spent copious amounts of warm cum over my face and even into my eyes. I was dazed, and my mouth fucked senseless, not knowing what to expect next. Maybe a beating.

"Now, go home!" Ish ordered.

I struggled to my feet and looked back at them only once, still disorientated and coming down from my own orgasm and experience I didn't understand.

I began to run as fast as my aching knees would allow me. I reached Losberg Street, where many protestors I'd partied with dispersed. I shoved past them. Those who saw me coming jumped out of my way but must have noticed the spunk running down my face.

I didn't stop running until I reached our apartment. I tore through the door. That was when my understanding of the world as I knew it shattered.

I crashed inside, calling for Peter, and fell over the suitcases he had packed.

He stumbled out of his bedroom with wide eyes and bed hair and helped me up. "André, what happened to you?" he asked, concerned and struggling to get me up from the floor. It wasn't an easy task since he was smaller than me in height and weight. "Why do you smell like..."

Ashamed, I watched as he assessed my hair that had been grabbed and pulled, my face smeared with cum, and my well-used mouth. "Wait, did you get attacked? I knew it. I told you we're not safe here!" He was referring to the Disciples sending men to punish us for being attracted to men instead of women.

I was scared of something totally different. I had been mouth-fucked by strange men who were surely not human or from here and somehow made themselves look like us, especially like my Peter!

A deep rumble and chuckles of an unwelcome visitor woke me from my hysterics. "We thought you would never get here," Ish said from the direction of the living room.

I pushed Peter back. "Get out, Peter, run!" But he didn't move.

"These two forced me to suck them off in an alley... they... are here to kill us. They're fucking hunting us. They know about us leaving!" I heaved for air and frantically pulled Peter to push him out the door, willing him to leave. The apartment was dark. No lights were on, and yet I somehow knew they saw us.

"They want both of us and asked about the Disciples." I turned to look in their direction. "Leave my friend alone, and I'll tell you everything about the Disciples," I said.

Peter resisted and wasn't moving. My body was shaking, and as soon as he heard me mentioning the Disciples, he flung himself around.

"Those right-winged hooligans think we live in the dark ages. They use intimidation and fear to achieve their ends. We want out, you hear me! We don't want anything to do with them! I will tell you anything you want to know. Can you help us?" Peter asked.

"We know, and that's why we're here," the other Peter said and chuckled, and the light in the living room came on.

Peter froze. He was stunned by the two handsome but dangerous-looking strangers, and one looked like him enough to be his twin. Inside the apartment with its low-hanging ceiling, Ish looked even bigger. Even though they'd just forced me to suck them, my cock stirred at the sight of them.

Other Peter chuckled. "No, I, we had enough for tonight, down, boy," he said as if reading my mind.

"You never said no. You enjoyed every minute of it," Ish said, and I wondered whether there was a time I could have said no. Yes, he did ask, only I'd never answered.

"We are here with a very important message and, of course, to help you," Ish said.

My Peter gasped and slammed both hands in disbelief over his mouth. "You... you... me... no! How can that be?" He pointed back and forth between himself and the other Peter. He must have thought it was him, and I stepped closer to take him in. It was dark in the alley, so here, next to each other in the light, there wasn't any fucking doubt in my mind. It was his double or a long-lost brother, I thought.

The other Peter answered in the same voice and same Bavarian accent, "Yes, it's me, and no, I'm not your brother or any other relative. My name is Peter." He lifted his sleeves, showing his wrists, the same wrists my Peter had slashed a month before. I found him bleeding out and trying to die because he was gay.

Since then, we have devised a plan to escape our fathers and the organization that has been ruling our families for generations.

"We know what you're planning with regard to getting on that train tomorrow, never to return. That train is going to be bombed by a right-winged communist. Only Peter will survive. You will never make it or escape to America. Let me help you, and..." Ish said, interrupted by my Peter hitting the floor passed out cold.

"Get a cold cloth, Ish," other Peter said and jumped to help as I scooped my Peter's head into my lap.

"Come on, be okay. I love you. I can't live without you," I cried as the night's oppressive, disorientating emotions flooded my system and broke my resolve. Tears streamed down my face as I remembered how close to death I found him just a month before, and now pale as a sheet again, reminding me how fucked-up our lives were.

"Here you are." Ish handed me a cold, wet rag.

I wiped over my Peter's forehead, his cheeks, and down to the back of his neck. "That's it, open your eyes," I coaxed.

And other Peter said, "Don't worry, you're fine. We're not here to hurt you. We need your help as much as you need ours," he said, smiling gently at my Peter and me. Not at all the motherfuckers from the alley.

"Tie your hair away so I can see your face," I ordered other Peter this time. He happily took his long blond locks and tied them with a leather string he produced from his pocket. Ish bent down to kiss him, and my mouth hung open.

"*Donnerwetter,*" my Peter whispered in German and passed out again. I wiped his face again until crystal blue eyes opened and looked up at us. The same blue eyes in the face of the man I sucked off in the alley. I knew both pairs of eyes very well. The other Peter's eyes were maybe a few years older, but not much.

"How is this possible?" I asked, continuing to wipe my Peter's face to soothe him.

Ish came closer, bent to one knee, and scooped my Peter up. "Come, let's put him on the sofa," he said gently, and I trusted him for some inexplicable reason.

Once my Peter had woken fully, they explained who Ish was. He was the last of his kind and not a vampire. He told us about a timeline he discovered and, so too, distant relatives and his lover, the other Peter. They knew about our fathers and the organization, the experimentation on us as fetuses, and explained that we were also distant relatives of Ish. His blood was the ancient bloodline of the Anunnaki who created humans and exited the earth at the fall of Babylonia, and it was they who left the gold cylinder engraved with the tree of life. Ish had been trying to rectify the demise of Earth, but the more he meddled, the worse it got. His family, the timeline the other Peter was from, had him swearing to stop fiddling and let it be. This was our timeline. He could visit with us and promised not to change the timeline and how things were when he met the other Peter in the future.

CHAPTER 10
JUANDRE

My eyes were wide open in surprise. "Holy shit. My head is spinning!" I exclaimed after finishing listening and trying to take it all in. "I need something stronger than milk." I jumped up from the table and rumbled around for anything. I found a half-empty bottle of Lord Andrew and put down a tumbler for each of us. Then, I sat back down and sipped the strong liquid burning my throat, feeling instantly relaxed and able to continue listening.

Andrew continued. "But when they said Anunnaki, my Peter lost it. He laughed and curled into a ball, rolling hysterically on the floor. It took my Peter and me a few hours to ask questions and listen to their adventures and explanations. The condensed version is that we were half relatives and needed to be given the gift, as Ish called it. He said the world was near ending as we knew it, and we had to be prepared. They handed us a list of things to collect and told us where to store it for our future selves. The biggest and weirdest request was whiskey. Hence, I own a whole bloody distillery. That will make a general and thousands of men very happy in the future. Peter is currently working undercover, and we grew apart. It wasn't until I met you that I truly felt something. It took me ten years to realize. But I'm here and only offering the bite if you truly want it."

"Tell me more. Why did they force you to suck them off in the alley?" I asked.

"I don't know," Andrew told me. "They didn't force me. I thought about it many times—and I think I didn't realize it was an S/m kink I have. When you picked me up and took me to the hotel in twenty-oh-four, I loved how you took control and the power-play we exchanged. They must have known the future me. They said they're from a time when only men walked the earth. When men were married, sometimes there were not just two but three, four, and even five men in a coupling. Their children are born without a living woman."

"No way!" I said with disbelieving wonder.

"Yes, and I can't wait to see it! That's what Peter is doing now. He's collecting and preparing eggs and technology to make it all possible."

"And the Disciples?" I asked, never missing a beat.

"We have them sorted. Ishtar and Peter don't want us to interfere too much with the timeline. Things still need to happen as they did, and we can make it easier and better by not fiddling too much, and Ish keeps track of them. They are..." Andrew stopped mid-sentence and frowned, looking like he wasn't ready to divulge something, so I didn't pry.

"So Ish and other Peter traveled in time? How? Where is your Peter?" I asked, changing the subject to more exciting things.

"It's always been possible for the royal family," Andrew explained. "Ish has a ship that can jump in time. He's the last member of the royal family of Anzulla. I have no clue where Anzulla is or if it's even in our solar system. It sounds like he's some time police or timekeeper."

"Really? A time-traveling Anunnaki, and not a vampire, but Anunnaki from Anzulla, is in love and traveling with the older Peter?" I asked as I put it all together, and after everything that had happened, I had no difficulty believing this.

Andrew nodded. "They told us that night that I never would have made it to America and that my Peter returned and continued his current work. That's why he had to go on doing his job and research. I was put on another train to escape the train crash, but my family believed I'd died in it because Peter told them I had run away and had taken that train destined to take me to America.

"When I arrived, I changed my name from André to Andrew, used my doctorate to create the perfect whiskey, and started Lord Andrew Distilleries. All the while, I monitored the organization's American chapter. I still talk to my Peter occasionally. Unfortunately, it's as if he's lost interest, and his work has become everything to him. I think he's just going through the motions while waiting for Ish."

I jumped up. "Okay, I don't want to waste another bloody minute. Bite me, drink me, and then fill me up," I said with vigor and slammed my hand on the table, eager to get this ball rolling.

"Are you sure about this? Do you want me to bite you and spend the rest of your life with me?" Andrew asked.

I put my hands on his hips and answered him with a smoldering gaze. Then, so he knew I was super sure, I nodded and smiled.

Andrew's fangs peeked over his bottom lip, and I thought I was also falling in love with them, too. He looked adorable when they were extended. His eyes sparkled with a green sheen. Although he didn't like the word vampire, he was a stunning teddy bear. I saw myself waking up beside his magnificent beauty and in those strong arms daily. *Easily*.

"Your place is equipped for protection, so I guess living there with you is the smart option, but it's a bit far from my work. Where would we live? Should I find a job closer to the distillery? And what about Charlie?" I asked Andrew.

Andrew jerked his head up and stared at me with an intense look, and I forgot what else I wanted to say. "Don't worry about those details now," he told me. "They will sort themselves out."

Neither of us broke eye contact with each other as I took Andrew's hand, led him to the sofa, sat him down, and climbed on his lap. Slowly I massaged his cock with the palm of my hand.

"If you suck me, I'll suck you," he pleaded with a promise.

"I'll suck you even if you don't suck me, but then you won't have a friend to spend eternity with," I said seductively.

Andrew sighed, and it sounded like relief as he

plopped his head back, and his breathing became faster.

"Do you need oxygen like everyone else? Why else would you breathe?" I kept my voice low and teasing. The bulge beneath my hand grew in size and firmness. I lowered the zipper on Andrew's pants slowly, freeing him, and kept leisurely rubbing his stiffness while kissing him hungrily. His shaft was a solid rod of flesh, and at the first hint of pre-cum, I slipped my thumb over the slit, smearing it over his cock head.

I wanted to taste Andrew badly, so I released the kiss to slide down and sit back on my heels. Bending forward, I tasted the sweet taste of Andrew's arousal, and it was exquisite. I wanted more.

I slid my lips over his cock, and then licked all around the head. Slipping my tongue into the slit, I delved deeper for more of his sweet nectar. Next, I relaxed my throat and swallowed him to the root so his pubes tickled my nose. Andrew's breath hitched, and he swore obscenities and grabbed hold of my hair, holding me in place. I closed my eyes, enjoying his taste, while I listened to Andrew panting and begging for more and not to stop.

To prolong his pleasure, I drew back. "Baby, I haven't even started yet."

Andrew's dazed eyes popped open as he lifted his head. He stared down at me, his pupils blown, and it seemed like he forgot to speak. He opened and closed his mouth, then plopped his head back again.

I dug my fingers into the sides of Andrew's hips and squeezed hard.

"Lie down," I ordered, and Andrew hissed through his fangs but fell obediently to the side, surrendering. I moved my hands to his tight, muscled butt and grabbed hold of the thick blanket of hair covering them.

"Close your eyes," I told him. "Only feel. I love your hairy body. You're built like a mountain man and move with the swagger of a lion. You're all my man, and you smell so good."

Andrew rolled his head from side to side in answer to my loving him with words and hands, surrendering to my touch.

"I'm yours. Do with me as you please," Andrew whispered in a whine while lisping the *please*, begging me to do more to him.

I sucked the head of his cock through tight lips, knowing exactly how it felt, then swallowed him down again. Arching his back, Andrew hissed and groaned his pleasure. I continued moving my mouth up and down, getting his cock as wet as possible.

Andrew's eyes opened, and we glanced at each other. Again, he seemed to want to say something, thought better of it, and gave up. I smiled around his thick cock and loved the solid feel in my mouth.

"I want to bite you," he slurred like a bear waking up from slumber.

I scraped my teeth over his shaft and let his cock fall with a plop out of my mouth. I tore my gaze away from the beautiful thing and grinned at Andrew.

"Today is the first day of the rest of our existence together," I said and rubbed my face in the fuzziness of Andrew's lower belly and pubic hair and moved down to where his member lay, twitching for attention. Shudders coursed through Andrew, and it seemed he liked the soft, sensual caresses just as much as the painful ones. Good to know because I loved finding out new ways to pleasure him.

Sliding my tongue down, first the left and then the right side of his iliac furrows, I reached behind to grab his buttocks, squeezing hard. His engorged cock leaked a drop of pre-cum, and I suckled the tip, teasing him.

"Please, Juandre, for love of, just do something," he begged.

I glanced up. "Something wrong, lover?"

Andrew gave me a mock death glare. In answer, I flicked the head with my tongue. The heavy, blood-filled organ twitched. In a deliberate, slow circle, I swept my tongue around the head and asked, "Is that better?" Then, I kissed my way down along his shaft and grabbed Andrew's balls, pulling them and rolling them in the palm of my hand.

"Yes, just like that. Hmmm, that feels amazing," Andrew muttered.

"I think it's time," I said. Like a predator taking notice of his prey, Andrew's eyes shot open, and he watched himself being climbed like a tree, never breaking eye contact with me.

"I'm going to ride you while you bite me. Is that okay?" I asked because I wasn't sure if blood was going to get on my furniture or not.

Andrew swallowed audible gulps, his Adam's apple bobbing up and down, while I removed the last of our clothes and slid back up him. "Are you going to drink me dead and turn me like the movies, slash your wrist, and let me suck on it?"

"No, it's not like the movies, and I'm not a vampire!" Andrew chuckled as I straddled him, holding myself up on my knees, my cock touching his.

"Then what are you, if not a vampire?" I needled

as I squared his cock up with my hole and reached one hand back to fondle his balls. "You have a sun allergy, fangs, drink blood, and sleep during the day. You're fast and strong, and you smell perfect. You can read minds and plant ideas. Of course, you're a vampire. What else would you be?"

"I'm a superhuman with Anunnaki DNA," Andrew said as he pushed his hips upward, trying to push his cock head into my tight hole. He grunted as I teased him by moving away, and he added, "I was gifted these powers from a royal-blooded Anunnaki. And no, all I have to do is mate and bite you, after which I inject whatever is in my venom into you. I only have enough for one bite, for my mate. You have to bond with me in the same way. We will then become a bonded pair, much like a marriage; the only difference is that we can't divorce. We must die to break the bond, either together, which is prefer-able because if one leaves the other behind, the remaining one would wish they had died, as we won't be able to live without each other. You'll have enough for one bite, so you need to be sure that I'm the one you want to spend eternity with. After the sac is drained, it doesn't refill. That's what Ishtar told me."

"I wish I could meet your Ishtar. He sounds like…

hmmm," I moaned as I pushed back against his cock head and then pushed downward, inwardly smiling, knowing I was the one giving Andrew his pleasure and that he'd waited and wanted me all this time. Warmth flooded through me as I pushed down, and he pushed up, holding onto my hips. I was very sure it was love. I wanted to spend an eternity with this man, with this vampire. Whether he thought he was one or not. Andrew's teeth were over my jugular, biting. Scorching hot pain and pleasure shot through me as Andrew wrapped both arms around me, holding me in place. I couldn't move. Sparks flew before my eyes, but only our howls of pain and pleasure filled the living room. Suddenly, I felt weaker and sleepier, and then it all went black as I passed out and lost consciousness.

CHAPTER 11
ANDREW

IT'S BEEN TWENTY-FOUR HOURS SINCE I HAD GIVEN Juandre my mating bite. With giddy optimism, I stepped from the cloud of bellowing steam following me from the ensuite bathroom and tied my terry cloth belt loosely around my waist with twitchy fingers. I patted the side pocket to make sure my surprise was still there. The steam mixed and disappeared in the soft yellow light as it cut through it like sunlight would cut through the early morning mists of a rainforest. My gaze roamed over the scene and drank in the breathtaking sight before me.

"You know I've always dreamed of you waiting in our bed for me, but this sight before me, I could never have imagined, is so much better," I said.

Juandre lifted the red satin sheet off his body, pushing it aside and spreading his legs so I could see his balls already pulled up and the dark silhouette of his cock straining against the white-laced briefs. Juandre reached slowly inside and freed his cock from its sexy confinement, and palmed his erection —stroking it until a bead of pre-cum appeared at the tip.

My mouth watered. I wanted to lick it. My pointy incisors lengthened and pushed over the round bow of my bottom lip. My gaze wandered over Juandre's olive skin and drank in the perfect form of his body. The matching white lace top of his nightie softly draped over his well-defined pecs, and the dark, prominently pointed hard nubs of his nipples called to me to bite them. The lace ruffled over the chest hair that trailed down over the hills and valleys of his abdominal muscles and stopped right above the neatly trimmed dark bush surrounding his impressively thick eight-inch cock. I didn't stop my gaze there and let it trail further down his long, sexy thighs, ending at his beautifully pedicured red toes. He was stunning, even more so now that he'd taken my bite. I had to remind myself to take a few deep breaths.

"Do you like it?" Juandre purred seductively and

thrust up into his hand. His eyes were dark with lust, and self-confidence oozed while he rubbed the loose lace over his chest and abdomen.

"My dream has finally come true," I muttered, moving closer. "Here you are in my bed, dressed in your sexy lace nighties, just for me, and so hungry for sex. And we're both vampires. I wished for this so many times. To make love and to be touched, without secrets between us." *I'd better get on with it,* and my heart thundered in my chest. When I reached the bed, I dropped to one knee, took the surprise out of my pocket, and held up a small blue and silver-colored box, like an offering, to Juandre.

Juandre was up and at the edge of the bed in an instant. Gripping the edge tightly, he swung his feet over to the floor. "Andrew, what is this?" he asked, eyes wide with amazement.

I loved the high lilt in Juandre's surprised voice. I loved everything about this man. I wanted to spend eternity with him.

"Juandre, please let me do this," I urged him, our gazes locked.

Biting his lip, Juandre nodded.

"You know, I loved you from the moment I first saw you. When you stopped your red *Porsche* next to me on the I-seventy-five, my heart broke instantly because I was convinced you could never return my feelings. I thought you were happy and you had your whole life planned out. You were on your way to becoming a doctor, and the longer we fucked that weekend, the more I wanted you. I played into your fantasy, never realizing it was mine, too. Although we parted physically, my mind couldn't part ways with you. You stole my heart and soul, and the longer we spent time apart, the more your smile and face taunted me. Every day without you was filled with loneliness and bitterness. I experienced such hopeful joy when I learned we lived in the same town." I stroked my trembling fingers over Juandre's plump bottom lip. "I wasted so much time. I was such an idiot. For ten years, I suffered, not knowing you suffered, too."

Juandre reached out, took my hand, and held it. Squeezing as if to say, *I hear you go on*.

"The company was never meant to see what I felt for you. I was determined to keep my private life and feelings locked away. I was afraid of losing my respectability and control over them. I built Lord Andrew from the ground up and saved it for a future that has yet to come. I was scared of losing you and the company. Never realizing it's bloody mine, that we're stronger together, and no one can take either away from me. You opened my eyes and unlocked the cage I built for myself and hid inside. From love, from you, Juandre. I know all this has been a tornado of change for you. The way you handled it and accepted it still takes my breath away. You're so much more than I expected. I hope I'm worthy of you. Just being with you, how your mind works, and how you calculate every next step amazes me. I want to be with you as much as I want to fuck you."

Juandre chuckled and leaned closer, his breath washing over my face. He smiled and looked down. at the box in my hand as he opened it, revealing the glowing blue band Ish had given me to give my husband one day. "It was made from metal that has not yet been discovered," I said, and an intake of breath made me look at Juandre, who stared at the ring.

"It's a gift from my friends. I told you you'll meet those who visited and turned me in the future. It's a metal that glows blue at night, and apparently, they built spaceships from it. It's our secret. I love you and wanted to know if you would agree to marry me one day when it is legal. But until then, and after that, I will serve you and love you as best I can."

Juandre pulled me closer, tears in his eyes and

smiling. "Are you putting the ring on my finger, or should I do it myself?" he asked.

"Don't be impatient. We have eons ahead of us." Happiness and excitement shot through me as I pushed back my tears of joy that were choking me. "Juandre, will you spend the rest of your life with me? Will you marry me as soon as we're able?"

Juandre wrapped his right hand around the back of my neck and offered his left hand for me to slip the ring onto his finger. I realized he was still waiting for me and hurriedly took the glowing ring out of the box, throwing the box somewhere over my shoulder, and slipped the ring onto a smiling Juandre's finger. His glistening white little fangs pushed down his bottom lip. He was still getting used to them but looked so cute with them.

His turning yesterday had been easy and highly erotic. I had penetrated him, and we made love through the whole ordeal, just like Ish had turned me all those years ago. Being a royal family member from Anzulla, each family member had a special gift, which could only be passed on to one special person. Ish had given his gift to me because Peter didn't need it.

Almost half a century later, one year ago, Ish handed me the ring and told me to search for my mate, make whiskey, and one day save the earth and, ultimately, the universe.

Yes, we did drink blood, but we also ate and drank everything we used to. The high protein concentrations of globulins in the blood were what we needed to survive. The human liver and immune system make globulins, which our bodies need to fight cell breakdown and infections. That is why we drank blood.

"I'd like it if we could play a game tonight," Juandre said with a lisp through his new incisors. His cock pointed at me and bobbed a few times on its own. Like saying, *here I am; come get me*. "Hmmm, let Daddy make you feel good tonight," Juandre said as he grabbed the bottle from the bedside table and applied a generous amount to two fingers. "Get on your hands and knees, boy," he ordered.

I immediately switched to being submissive and unrobed, then did what I was told to do.

Juandre carefully rubbed lube around my entrance. "Hmmm, you feel ready for your Daddy tonight. You're such a good boy, aren't you?" he asked as he twisted one finger inside me, pumping that finger slowly. He worked it in, hitting my prostate. He knew exactly how to rub my pleasure button.

"You were so good, asking Daddy to marry you. I'm proud of you for showing courage and your love." He pulled back, and one finger was joined by many more. The discomfort was unexpected, but I enjoyed it and wouldn't protest.

I'll let Daddy do whatever he wants to me. I trust him and can't wait to feel what he sticks into me tonight.

"Ahh, Daddy, that feels so good! Thank you, Daddy," I whined, sinking deeper into my role.

"You deserve everything I'm going to give you. Just enjoy this, my boy. Just enjoy," Juandre coaxed.

"Ahh," I moaned, and my eyes rolled back in my head. Juandre worked his fingers in and out of me for a long time. His fingers glided over my prostate with precision, and I sucked in breath after breath. I moaned and rocked my ass back and forth for more.

Juandre pulled his fingers out. And the feeling of emptiness had me begging, "No, Daddy, please don't stop. I was so close. I need more, please, Daddy." I felt more lube drizzling over my ass. Juandre was doing an enthusiastic job of lubing me so well that it dripped down my aching balls.

"I see you washed yourself out for Daddy, didn't you? You expected to be used well tonight?" He gave his approval, revving my motor higher.

"Ah, yes, just for you. I wanted you, Daddy," I

admitted because I did. I then felt what could only be something huge. It stretched me so wide I thought it would tear me open. *It must be a coned sex toy.*

"Daddy!" I yelled in surprise.

"Take it. I know you can," Juandre purred and moved the cold thing back. I wanted to look, but I enjoyed the sensation too much. It drove my endorphin levels sky-high, and bliss washed over me.

Then I felt Juandre getting up from the bed as the mattress dipped this and that way. I heard rummaging in the closet and ripping and crunching of paper bags. "Wow, Daddy, are you getting more toys? You're going full throttle on my ass," I said, needing him to bring whatever he had and fuck me.

"Lift your chest," Juandre ordered, and I did. Juandre lay three pillows in front of me. "Okay, lie down. Thank you. You're such a good boy, but I need you to feel, with no questions and no looking."

I was delirious with happiness. I loved him fucking me so much. "Yes, Daddy," I said and lay down, making myself comfortable.

Next, Juandre tied my hands to the bedpost and applied a spreader to my ankles. I could probably break out of them, but the illusion made Juandre happy, and that made me happy.

"Oh, my fucking shit!" I howled into the mattress. Juandre had poured something extremely hot, no, not hot, it was cold and yet not cold, into my ass. "What are you doing? You're burning my insides. I can't take it," I exclaimed. Juandre purred and kept massaging it deeper into me until his entire fist was worked into my channel. Pumping it rhythmically back and forth while his other hand rubbed my balls and cock with the hot and cold lube. They were on fire! I was jelly.

"Feels good, doesn't it?"

"It burns."

"Are you sure you're burning?"

I stopped and concentrated. *No, it wasn't burning. It was tingling!*

"You want your Daddy to stop?" Juandre asked me gently, moving his hand from my cock and balls and up onto my back.

"No, sorry, Daddy, I'm ridiculously stupid."

"That's okay. Daddy wanted that to happen, don't worry. Daddy will only do things that are safe for you. You can tell Daddy to stop anytime."

"Okay, yes, please, Daddy, don't stop," I said, feeling Juandre remove his hand and move in behind me. Then I heard something sprayed out of a can, and warm hands massaged it over my well-stretched hole.

"Hmmm, tastes so good," Juandre said, and I relaxed. Whatever he doused me with smelled sweet. My vampire senses told me that Juandre was busy with cream and chocolate.

When he was done, I was a lump of relaxed, lustful flesh, just lying there enjoying it. Juandre lay down on top of my back.

"I've always wanted to lick cream and chocolate from your beautiful body," he said lovingly in my ear and thrust his cock inside me.

The pleasure was intense. "Oh yeah," I moaned. "Daddy's cock's just right for hitting my good spot."

"Okay, baby boy. Daddy's going to fuck you. Daddy needs to get his cock deep inside you!" Juandre started power fucking me harder than I ever remembered being fucked, and I realized it was because he had vampire strength now. We reached our first orgasm fast and were cheering with satisfied, impressed grunts when our cocks swelled, and Juandre filled me again and again.

"Yes, Daddy, fill my hole!" I begged.

Juandre obliged, and when we orgasmed for the fourth time, we were a sticky mess—drenched with sweat and sated when Juandre finally rolled off me.

Short of breath, he heaved as he said, "I should untie you and get you in the shower, boy."

I didn't say a word. I had been totally and inexplicably fucked and sucked. Instead, I grunted in agreement with a shower. Juandre untied me and rubbed life back into my wrists and arms.

We bonded and became a vampire couple after we repeated the mating words that Peter and Ishtar had taught me.

> "*Mates in love, we'll weather life's storms,*
> *holding tight to each other's memory.*
> *Our bond will never falter or break,*
> *for our love is pure and strong.*
> *With or without you by my side, our love can conquer anything,*
> *for you are my strength and my everything.*
> *Mates in love until the end of time,*
> *forever bonded in heart and mind.*"

Marriage to Juandre was going to be awesome!

"Can't wait to marry you. How do you feel about a marriage and honeymoon in South Africa?"

"I think I fucked you senseless. Why South Africa?"

"That's where I store the whiskey for Ishtar. I

want to take you and Charlie on a safari and show you the big five in their natural habitat." I looked into those sparkling chocolate brown eyes that looked so lovingly back at me.

"That sounds adventurous, and adventure is my middle name," Juandre said, kissing me.

Our hearts were full of deep love for each other. He was my mate. I should never have waited so long to find him. But we have an eternity together.

"We can have a small ceremony. I'll ask Tony to get the paperwork ready. What do you say?"

"Of course, it sounds perfect!"

CHAPTER 12
JUANDRE

THE CAPTAIN'S VOICE, SMOOTH AND DEEP, FILLED THE cabin. "This is your captain speaking. We're beginning our descent into Carletonville and anticipate landing around 8:25 PM, about ten minutes early. Local time is 7:45 PM if you wish to adjust your watches. The weather there is hot, with some overcast, and a temperature of 32 degrees Celsius. On behalf of the entire crew, we hope you enjoy your visit, and we look forward to seeing you again, Lord Andrew." The announcement sparked a thrill of anticipation in me.

"God, why do they always call you Lord Andrew?" I murmured to my fiancé. He sat up straighter. "Because I *am* Lord Andrew," he answered, as if it were obvious. I rolled my eyes.

"You made that up, and now everyone's playing along like you're actually royalty," I muttered.

"Who says I'm not? Anyway, I don't have a last name. My last name *is* Andrew, so you should call me Lord next time you fuck me," he purred. The sweet smell of whiskey clung to his breath, and I suddenly wanted a taste. I was sure our metabolisms were in overdrive, considering we'd polished off nearly three bottles on the flight.

"I'm not falling for that," I chuckled, leaning closer to whisper in his ear, "You're *my* boy." Andrew inhaled sharply, his green eyes darkening, swirling with alluring thoughts. I could stare into those eyes forever. "And I'm not changing my last name to Andrew," I added.

He wrinkled his nose. "I figured you wouldn't want to. You'll always be Juandre Martinez to me."

I submitted my resignation on the way to Andrew's private airstrip outside Lexington. Meanwhile, Andrew picked up Charlie and Tony while handling the paperwork for our marriage license and entry visas for South Africa.

Thankfully, Lord Andrew Whiskey was quite popular in South Africa, so Tony only needed to make two calls, and that's how we ended up here. While I locked up the house and said my goodbyes, Andrew and Charlie were getting acquainted. After nearly twenty-four hours of flying with just a refueling stop in Algeria, I finally joined them at midnight.

Our lives were changing drastically, and I embraced it—a clean slate. It felt like I'd been waiting for this my whole life, as if it were meant to be. And now that I have Charlie and Andrew, that's all I need.

Andrew asked, as if he could read my mind.

I leaned in to kiss his soft lips. "Yes, I'm ready!" I said, turning to Charlie across the aisle. "Are you all strapped in? Let me help you stow your things."

We began sorting through the trash. "I can't believe you brought so many electronics. A laptop, a tablet, a cellphone, an MP3 player... hopefully, you'll be so busy meeting new people that you won't even need these," I said, knowing I was irritating him. He hated being fussed over about his screen time, but I helped anyway, folding up his table and handing him his backpack. This wasn't his first time on a jet; his mother and grandparents often flew to exotic places. As a trauma surgeon, I never had time for that. But now I have Charlie and Andrew, my soon-to-be husband, and considering I now have fangs I struggle to keep hidden, working with blood isn't in my best interest.

"I don't think I'm leaving the hotel. It's not safe in South Africa, Dad." Charlie shoved his belongings into his backpack, and I took it from him, repacked it, and placed it in the overhead compartment. He was tired and irritated after flying around the globe for the past week.

Andrew said that while I was sleeping, just as he turned me into a vampire, my father had called. He mentioned Chrissy had an accident and that Charlie wanted to come home to me. His mother was that way, and I'm happy to have my boy here with us.

Something else happened. Charlie said he never wanted to talk about it. I tried to phone my father to find out what had happened, but they weren't answering their phones.

Andrew said he must have been asleep because when Tony arrived at the villa, my father pushed Charlie into his arms and told him to take care of the boy; his mother could not look after him.

My father did the first selfless thing by sending Charlie home to me. Andrew had said that, with time, Charlie might want to talk, and I agreed. As long as Charlie was with me, I was sure he would be happy and speak to me when he was ready.

"Andrew really knows the area, and it's not a hotel. We're staying at a guest house on a wildlife reserve," I said to my grumpy son, his hair a mess. Charlie crossed his arms, drew his legs up to his chest, and stared out the window. "I know, Andrew told me. I just forgot," he muttered, scowling. "And I don't need any new friends."

fine, it doesn't matter. What matters is we're together. We should talk about your mother–"

"I don't care about her! I don't want to talk about them," Charlie interrupted, groaning.

I reached out to touch his shoulder, but jumped when the captain's announcement boomed from the speaker above. "Gentlemen, we've begun our descent into Carletonville. Please secure your carry-on items, stow your tray tables, and hand any remaining service items or unwanted reading materials to the flight attendants. Kindly turn off and stow all portable electronic devices until we disembark. To prepare for landing, please return your seat backs to their upright position and fasten your seat belts, asking your flight attendant for assistance if needed. Thank you."

Charlie jumped up. "I need the washroom!"

"Yes, quick," I said, snapping my fingers. Charlie

grabbed the headrest, lifted his feet, and shot out of his seat.

I turned to Andrew. "I need to use the restroom!" I said, gesturing toward the blinking green lavatory light. Andrew gave me an encouraging look, then passed our empty glasses to an attendant nearby.

John, one of the more attractive flight attendants, came over with a warm smile. "We'll be landing in about thirty minutes, sir, so you have plenty of time," he said, stepping out of my way. He was striking, with dark, kind eyes and perfectly coiffed hair. I couldn't help but notice his impeccably shaped eyebrows when he spoke.

"Good to know. I just need to get a few things," I replied, remembering I wanted to freshen up. I went back to my seat to grab my small bag and a clean shirt I had set aside. Grinning at Andrew, I added, "I'll be right back." He just shook his head, amused.

"Slow down. You're moving at vampire speed," he murmured.

"Shit, sorry," I shrugged, batting my eyelashes innocently. Then I turned and moved in slow motion.

John was still waiting for me. He waved me down the aisle. "I'm so sorry about the mess my boy made. I was just about to clean it up," I apologized as he started picking up the clutter Charlie had scattered around his sofa bed.

"No problem at all. This is my job, sir," he said, friendly.

"Alright then," I whispered and began heading toward the large, luxurious washroom at the far end of the jet.

CHAPTER 13
ANDREW

"CARE FOR ANOTHER DRINK, SIR?" THE FLIGHT ATTENDANT inquired, drawing my attention from Juandre's interactions with Charlie. Unbeknownst to him, I'd caught glimpses of his fangs at least twice during their conversation. I suspected Juandre could handle the truth about his ex-wife and father's murders, along with the deaths of the American and Italian Disciples. However, that would require confessing to wiping his memory and revealing that Charlie was his brother, not his son—so I maintained the facade. Someday, when the moment is right, I'll tell him everything—if that moment ever arrives. For now, their ignorance is their protection. But those fangs... I'm good at keeping secrets, but with Juandre, I'll give it another day—then Charlie will be informed.

I passed him our tumblers. "No, thank you. We've had plenty. Thank you for the wonderful service. Once we land, you and the crew can enjoy a Lord Andrew Platinum."

His face lit up. Those bottles go for over five thousand dollars apiece in the States. "Oh, thank you, sir, that's very kind of you."

"Come on," I said, "you can't tell me you don't like whiskey."

He flushed. "It's against policy, sir. We aren't permitted to accept gifts or gratuities from customers."

"Nonsense. What do you think I brought a whole case on board for? It's for you and the crew." He frowned, and I realized he must be new. "Don't worry, I'll tell the captain I said you could share it. He won't mind. The captain and copilot often fly for me."

He smiled, looking a little embarrassed. "Okay, thank you, sir," he replied.

"You're very welcome."

I glanced at Juandre, who signaled he was going to the restroom. "Sure, go ahead," I said with a smile and a nod. A moment later, Juandre was beside me, collecting his belongings.

I chuckled. "Slow down, you're going at vampire speed."

"Shit, sorry," he replied. Arms laden with toiletries and fresh clothes, he carefully backed up, turned, and made his way slowly to the back of the jet. If Charlie weren't here, I would have followed.

Amused, I watched his tight behind as he shuffled to the rear. Juandre disappeared into the restroom, and I settled back, contemplating our new family dynamic.

As Charlie returned to his seat, I smiled and waved. He waved back, and I turned my attention to the hum of the plane, anticipating our wedding night.

CHAPTER 14
JUANDRE

The South Africans were incredibly friendly and welcoming. There was a real buzz about the place, and most people seemed ambitious and happy to lend a hand. They were enthusiastic, genuine, and always ready with a smile or a laugh. Charlie quickly made friends with a local boy and girl his age, and within the reserve, we couldn't have asked for more, making wonderful memories together.

The only inconvenience was that the local municipality's electricity and water had been cut off daily at intervals—a practice known as Load Shedding. This was a side effect of corrupt government officials who did not reinvest taxes in the community but instead lined their own pockets by building extravagant palaces for themselves. As a result, there was no infrastructure or maintenance, but high crime rates. Each municipality had its own schedule across the country—something I had been unaware of. They were gradually slipping back into the dark ages, unfortunately, because Andrew had said that the country was handed over to the current government in pristine condition, so no kudos there.

Fortunately, the guesthouse on the wildlife reserve had its own water tank and electricity generators, which ensured that showers and meals ran smoothly. The sun had just set behind the blue backdrop of hills and valleys, painting the clouds with bright yellow and pink outlines, creating the impression of tongues of flames.

Charlie and I sat in the back seat of the old, rusted, white, doorless Jeep Wrangler with its roof open. Andrew sat next to the driver, scanning the tall grass for lions like us. So far, we had only seen a herd of zebras and antelope. Our driver and wildlife guide, Saul, a local Black man with an extremely long rifle beside him, promised us that a nighttime excursion would be just as exciting as a daytime one. Up until then, I couldn't say it had been fun. Charlie and I were terrified. God, a lion could have been stalking us, and we wouldn't have known until it was too damn late. We held each other's hands, glancing left and right over our shoulders, looking like helpless prey.

"Lion landscapes are perfect for these large carnivores to thrive," our guide said, with eyes more on us than the road. "Dad, we're going to be eaten! We're in their perfect landscape," Charlie exclaimed, and I concurred.

Saul drove while speaking up into the air, his voice booming into the darkness. "Today, African lions are limited to a few isolated regions. The Crocodile Wildlife Reserve, for example, holds just eight percent of South Africa's historical lion numbers. This shrinking habitat is largely due to illegal hunting and habitat loss. More than half of the remaining wild lions live alongside people and livestock in unprotected areas. For lions and other large carnivores to survive, their conservation must benefit the communities that live with them. That's why we work with local communities and partners to create spaces where both large carnivores and residents can prosper."

"Why is this reserve named after the crocodile? Are there more crocodiles than lions?" I asked, pointing toward the small river we had just crossed. "How far do crocodiles roam from the water?"

"Dad, I'm not getting out of this truck unless

that guy parks it in my bedroom so I can climb into bed," Charlie declared. Our guide chuckled. "That's a first for me! Don't worry; crocodiles won't eat you. It's the lions you should be worried about. They will track your scent and hunt you down," he added with a laugh.

Andrew gave the man a friendly slap on the shoulder. They were having a private conversation. I craned my neck to listen, but I couldn't catch anything.

"For God's sake, can't you see we're scared, and you're making it worse!" I shouted as I wrapped my arms around my boy. Andrew and Saul burst into laughter.

"No worries, I have a tranquilizer. I'll make them sleep before he can bite your head off your shoulders," Saul said, whispering something to Andrew.

"You'd better get us out of here if we're attacked, or *I'll* bite your head off!" I said, narrowing my eyes. Once again, Andrew and Saul whispered. I chose not to make a fuss about it; if push came to shove, I would grab Charlie and run. I was a vampire; I had tested my speed, and I could outrun a lion if I had to.

We drove for another minute, and then Saul began to speak again. The rhythm of his voice was soothing, and I could sense Charlie relaxing as our gazes wandered over the grasslands. He started pointing out various things, such as warthogs and even a large leopard tortoise he had spotted nibbling on the vegetation at the road's edge. The tortoise was clearly used to people, and the sound of our cameras clicking didn't scare it away.

"Alright, everyone, quiet down. We have a visitor," Saul announced. Charlie gasped, and then the truck lurched. My heart leaped into my throat as a lioness suddenly jumped down through the open roof. I stammered, almost shouting, but the sound caught in my throat. "Stay calm, Juandre; she won't hurt you. She's tame," Andrew reassured me.

"I think I just crapped my pants," I managed to whisper, my lips barely moving. My plan to rescue Charlie and escape had just gone out the window because the enormous purring beast now had its head nestled right between us.

"Stroke her neck and sides; she likes that," Saul whispered back. "She's a good girl. We rescued her when she was just a twelve-week-old cub and raised her by hand. She roams free now, and we think she'll be a momma soon."

"Dad, this is so cool!" Charlie whispered, rubbing the big cat so hard that dust puffed into the air.

"I wanted to surprise you. Her name's Passiony. I've known her since she was a cub and have seen her a few times since," Andrew explained.

"Yeah, this is definitely a surprise."

"Thanks to Andrew, we can afford to save more cubs like Passiony," Saul explained. She stepped back, and the truck tilted as she jumped out, then back in when Saul called, "Come here, girl, say hello." Andrew chuckled as the lioness nudged her large head against his neck, trying to climb into his lap. "Andrew, do you donate to this reserve?"

Saul chuckled at my remark, nudged Passiony aside, and gestured towards the bushes, indicating it was time to leave. She paused briefly, then jogged into the foliage. "Andrew is my boss. He pays our salaries." Saul then put the truck in gear.

"Wow, Andrew, that's incredible!" Charlie exclaimed, clearly impressed by the evening's surprise.

"I try my best to give back to this community. This land means a lot to me. It's not mine, it belongs to the people who work here. It's all held in trust, so everyone's an owner and their own boss," Andrew explained, tapping Saul's shoulder. "Thanks for showing my family around. I wasn't sure Passiony would make it; she took longer than last time."

"Yes, it takes her longer and longer to appear each time. One day, she won't show. That's how we'll know she's become a mother and is guarding her cubs," Saul explained, turning the car around.

Andrew leaned over the seat to speak with us. "We call this place Crocodile Wildlife Reserve because crocodiles were the first animals we rescued from a restaurant here, along with antelopes and other wildlife."

"Dad, you should marry this man tonight! He's so cool!" Charlie exclaimed excitedly, and I blinked in surprise.

Andrew turned back around. "Yes, we are getting married tonight. It's all arranged."

"What! Wait! No, no, no, no, no! We need cake and a pastor!" I cried.

Charlie covered my mouth with his hand. "Yes! Andrew asked me earlier if he could marry you, and I said it was okay."

"No problem! We'll get right on it as soon as we're back at camp," Saul said with a firm nod.

I glanced at Charlie. I had never seen him so happy. My son was beaming. "I guess we are getting married then!"

EPILOGUE
ANDREW

WE GOT MARRIED WITHOUT ANY FUSS. IT WAS JUST THE three of us, Tony and his crew. The staff at the Crocodile Inn, where I usually stayed when visiting my secret subterranean warehouse, quickly organized an early evening venue for us. I was impressed by Juandre's organizational skills. Within minutes, he had arranged the pastor and the cake, and within the hour, the ceremony began. The pastor signed our pre-approved papers to make it official, and then we wiped his memory before Tony took him back home. We kept our last names the same to avoid raising suspicion or attracting unwanted attention back home. Charlie didn't like the idea of exploring a mineshaft, so he stayed at the guest house with his new friends while I went to share my whiskey operation with my new husband.

My fingers nervously clutched and unclutched Juandre's hand. I was excited to show him where the whiskey I produced was stored for the future. That was why Ishtar made me a vampire, an Anunnaki consort, to hoard whiskey. I would educate him about the bloody Nosferatu the day I saw Ishtar again.

Deeper and deeper, we sank into the mineshaft I acquired in the 1980s.

"Oh wow!" Juandre exclaimed as the big steel door lifted and we stepped out of the elevator cage. "It's massive! I pictured us crawling through tunnels, but this is breathtaking. You could fit double-decker buses in here."

"We have a bus," I said with a proud smile. "It's not a double-decker, just a regular one." We watched the men use forklifts to move the crates deeper into the mine. Juandre's head turned from side to side.

His eyes widened as he stopped in his tracks. "No, seriously, how big is this?"

My heart skipped a beat. "So far, I have twelve warehouses in here as big as football fields."

Juandre hip-bumped me. "It's a whole city down

here. You own a city of whiskey. No wonder they call you Lord Andrew." I pulled him closer to kiss him. "Hmmm." Juandre moaned into my mouth and kissed me back. My head swirled with lust for him.

"Hello, Andrew."

What? Instinctively, I jumped in front of Juandre. A very tall, muscled man greeted me as though he knew me. He wiped his hands on the sides of his pants and extended a hand. I scowled at the man. I'd been bringing crates of whiskey for decades and had gotten to know everyone on my payroll pretty well.

I took his hand reluctantly, and we shook as I sized him up and down. "I'm sorry, I didn't catch your name. Are you new to the team?" I asked, searching Tony's face for recognition.

"No." The man shook Juandre's hand, stepped back, and slipped his hands into his back pockets, appearing relaxed. I didn't sense any strange vibes from him, but I didn't like the odd sensation in my gut or that strangers were hanging around. This was a secure, privately serviced area in the world's deepest mine. It was impossible to wander in here accidentally. I continued to scan him from head to toe. "I'm Gu. I'm an old friend of Ishtar's," the man said with a friendly demeanor.

"Ah!" I exclaimed, my face lighting up at the

mention of Ishtar. "Tony! He knows Ishtar," I said, nudging Tony closer. I felt safer with him by my side.

Tony offered a hand, and Gu shook it. "It's nice to meet a friend of Ishtar. I nearly shot you with my stun gun. How did you end up down here?" Tony asked what I'd been wondering about.

Gu smiled. He was attractive, with a light brown complexion and eyes that were a shade of yellow-green. His hair was dark and straight. He didn't look South African. "Those who know me call me the ghost of the land. I know you, Andrew, and Tony, too." He pointed at Tony. "I'm like him; I drank Ishtar's blood."

First, I frowned deeply, silently searching Gu's eyes for answers, and then it clicked. "So you're his Igigi?"

"Da, I'm supposed to be his best friend, but he forgot about me here. I've been wandering this land for hundreds of years, waiting for him," Gu said, and then the strange feeling I had made sense. He was one of us.

Tony and I burst into laughter. "Sorry, we're only laughing because that sounds exactly like something Ishtar would do." Gu gave a confirming grunt. "So where is he? If he's planning to come get me, he's too late, and my strength and time are finally running out." He shook his head.

"Oh, do you want some of my blood?" I asked, feeling sorry for him. Knowing that he was an Igigi of Ishtar instantly made him family.

"No, thank you. I'm tired and want to go to the other side. I'm almost a thousand years old. I've seen enough and tried my best to prevent the future. I've given up and told my son everything. It's in his hands now. If he were here, he would maybe be interested. But I doubt it. Thank you anyway. I came here today for the last time."

"Your son? Is he like us?" Tony and Juandre asked simultaneously, stepping closer and crowding the older man.

This was one of Tony's biggest worries. He wanted children. He'd been asking and researching vampire folklore without a definitive answer. "Ishtar rarely visited me. And when he does come, it's always some emergency. We never got time to sit down and discuss genealogy," I said with a chuckle, wondering what he was supposed to stop from happening.

"I met a woman and want to marry and have children with her." Tony pointed to me. "We didn't know if I could or if it was permitted," he said.

Gu smirked. I saw the exhaustion in his eyes. "Allowed, permitted?" He waved a don't care hand. "Who cares? Not Ishtar or Eryn! I would never have had a son if I had waited for their permission. Fuck permission. Do what you want. If you want one or twenty kids, have them. Life is changing constantly. Tomorrow, you wake up, and they are all gone. Don't wait. Do what you want. It doesn't matter what others say or think; the rules are what they are. Make your own bloody rules. I was lucky; a few years ago, I met my woman, and we had one son. I love her and want to be with her on the other side. My son is not Igigi, if that is what you are asking."

"Uhm, okay, thank you. That's good news." Tony said, happily satisfied and bowled over by Gu's bold answer.

Juandre lifted a finger. "One question, who the fuck is Eryn?"

Gu laughed. His voice curled around us, and a weird, uncomfortable feeling crawled up my spine. I froze, letting the feeling take over as I watched Gu with my jaw slack, and he started to draw something on the rocky wall with a piece of coal.

"It's all because of this," Gu whispered as he drew an apple.

We stood blinking. "An apple?"

"Da, a golden apple. If you ever come across it or Eryn here in the mine, destroy it." He drew a big X over the apple. This will prevent a big war very, very far into the future. Your past will disappear, and you won't have the blood of the Anunnaki."

"Huh?" We stood perplexed.

Gu waved again. "Bring your whiskey, but leave this sign with no golden apple for Eryn. If you see Ishtar, tell him I'm done with it all."

My eyes darted from Gu to Juandre. "What are you talking about? Where did you come from? You don't sound or look like someone from here?"

"I come from a time when the same war was fought repeatedly. Ishtar kept jumping and trying to win, but he lost. Over and over and over and over..." He trailed off.

"That's why you know us; you're from our future, and let me guess, Ishtar brought you here, and then you were lost, thinking he had forgotten about you."

"Yes!" Tony scoffed. "Yup, that's the same Ishtar we got to know very well."

"Ishtar told us not to do anything about the Disciples of the Anunnaki, but unfortunately, I had to eliminate an entire chapter in America.

"I know them. Kill as many of them as you can.

They are Zelk in the future. Like worms, they come from the apple. They are not here in Southern Africa. Not while I'm here. But they are coming. That is what I came for, to tell you."

Juandre laughed nervously. "Did you kill? When did you kill? Are you starting a war?" My blood froze. *Fuck!* How will I talk myself out of this? I'm not telling Juandre about his abduction. Not now. This is his happy honeymoon. I will tell him another day.

"I killed men from that organization I told you about. The Disciples of the Anunnaki. They are responsible for the science and research faculty at Humboldt University," I reminded him.

He pulled a face. "Yeah?"

"Baby, you have to understand, they are a scientism mafia group. They think they are the chosen of the Anunnaki. They are not. They are evil. It was either them or me."

Juandre crossed his arms. "Oh, so it was like self-defense?" he asked.

I took a deep breath to answer, but Tony spoke up. "Absolutely, self-defense." I raised an eyebrow at Tony, who shrugged innocently. I'll thank him for that later.

"Andrew, Juandre, and Tony, seeing your faces was great. I came to see the progress down here and to give you my message so Ishtar can stay away. Suppose he wants to stop the war. He should stay where he is, take his time machine apart, and never jump again."

"Got it! No jumping. Kill as many Disciples as we possibly can!" Juandre said, saluting Gu like a soldier. Tony gasped. I laughed awkwardly.

Gu nodded, crossing his arms in agreement. "Don't get me wrong, I love Ishtar, I really do. I can't imagine our world without him. But I've thought about him, about the Zelk's origin, and I've always come back to the same conclusion: it's all his fault. Him and his damn machine." He rubbed the back of his neck. "Many, many times."

"Zelk?"

"Da, they are the ones we were fighting, and there is no way of winning because they are tied to Ishtar and his fucking time machine."

"You say future, and then you say past. When did you come from, and what time period?"

"I have no idea. I came here from your future and my past when before the white man arrived here," Gu said.

"I was told in 1968 by Ishtar that important men will want whiskey in the future, and that's why we are hauling the stuff here," I said to Gu.

"Yeah, we had many parties and campfire stories with that whiskey. And yes, I guess the important men did enjoy it."

"At least I know I'm doing it right."

"Da! It was nice to shake your hand. I meant to come, but I wasn't ready to say hello or goodbye, and I will never see you again after today. I'm sure you understand when I say I just wanted a peaceful life with my wife and to raise my son. Once I married her, I gave up on Ishtar. Look me up. I worked as a history professor at the University of the Witwatersrand. Professor Gugusan Kilroy," he smiled with a naughty glint in his eye.

Of course, Juandre caught it first. "Don't tell me you are the famous Kilroy typically seen in graffiti? The *Kilroy was here* " became popular during World War II."

Gu thumbed his chest. "That's me, but I stole it. I thought it was funny at the time." Gu smiled and turned to leave. We stood watching his tight but ancient sexy ass as he disappeared into the darkness of the tunnels, with only a cool draft lingering.

THE END...

To be continued in Anzulla: According to ISH.

TIMELINE

Spoiler Alert!

New Beginnings M/M Series Timeline

Read or listen at your own risk.

25 000 B.C. Ishtar arrives at the San tribe.

25 000 B.C. Peter and Elijah jump to Anzulla.

24 970 B.C. Ishtar and Peter's crash landing.

24 970 B.C. The next day, Gugusan receives news that Ish is being held captive. Peter rescues Ishtar, thirty years after he had jumped with Elijah to Anzulla.

24 970 B.C. That night, Elijah and Peter arrive by boat at the San village. Peter gets his wings and brings the apple to the San.

24 970 B.C. Ishtar visits Anzulla, and Gugusan gives him the apple.

24 970 B.C. (Cian and his brothers arrived in Grayrak 93 A.T.) Ishtar slipped away to say goodbye to Gugusan and then met Peter for the first time.

23 000 B.C. Anzulla, Ishtar, receives a mission from the Fates.

3500 B.C. Hours before the war with Apsu, Ishtar and Peter bring the apple to Babylon. They rescue Elijah and seek help from Andrew in 2013 A.D., Ishtar, gives Andrew the wedding ring.

3500 B.C. Ishtar's story begins at age 250 years of age. He defeats his father for the first time during their uprising. *Anzulla, According to ISH: New Beginnings Book Three.*

1968 A.D. Young André (Andrew) and Peter meet Ishtar and older Peter. (No wings yet.)

2004 A.D. Juandre and Andrew's story begins. *Just like a Butterfly: A New Beginnings Novella.*

2013 A.D. Ishtar, Peter, and Elijah visit Lord Andrew Whiskey Distilleries, Lexington, Kentucky.

2014 A.D. Timeline Switch. Andrew goes to Juandre, they fall in love and mate. *Vampires Don't Drink Whiskey.*

2041 A.D. to 2043 A.D. (3-5 years before Doomsday.) Eryn and his brothers are born.

2046 A.D. DOOMSDAY. Worldwide breakout of Neurotoxic biochemicals. Nuclear Winter follows.

The story of the men of Phoenix begins - *Phoenix Code: New Beginnings Prequel.*

Ishtar arrives on the moon and waits for Cian, Ivan, and Eryn while guarding Barkor in Grayrak.

Then, after Ishtar meets Peter for the first time in Phoenix, 2146 A.D. (94 A.T.) he jumps back to 2046 A.D. to update Lasitor.

2051 A.D. (5 years after Doomsday.) The marriage of Mika and Connor takes place.

2052 A.D. (6 years after Doomsday.) The Big Flood (Tsunamis) happens, and, on that same day, the Romanov twins are born, marking it as the Year of the Twins: 0 A.T.

2058 A.D. (6 A.T.) The story of Eryn begins. *Eryn, King of the Brawl: New Beginnings M/M Series Part One.*

2073 A.D. (21 A.T.) Mika and Brad find the apple in the Disciples of the Anunnaki's confiscated loot. Cian and Ivan's Anunnaki heritage is revealed. Eryn makes each a sword of gold by dividing the forks on his trident so that they can focus their power on wrapping Phoenix in a protective layer to save their city from a string of global volcanic eruptions that led to the almost-instantaneous melting of the polar ice caps and global storms, turning Earth on its axis.

2124 A.D. (72 A.T.) Cian's first sighting of the hydrogen mining ship of the Zelk.

2145 A.D. (93 A.T.) Cian's story begins. *Cian's Song: New Beginnings M/M Series Part Two.*

2146 A.D. (94 A.T.) After finding and losing his mate, Ishtar meets Peter for the second time. This is also Peter's second meeting, but he had already met Ishtar back in 1968 A.D.)

Ishtar returns to Grayrak with Cian after meeting his Peter, grab his ship, jumps to Phoenix for a reboot, then returns to gather Peter to jump to 1968 A.D.

2147 A.D. (95 A.T.) Cian and his brothers evacuate Grayrak and take the last of the remaining humans with Barkor home to Phoenix. Rebirth of Earth's Timeline. Ishtar moves the Zelk to an alternate timeline to prevent them from attacking the Warship Horizon or Earth. Lots of shit goes down in this year!

2147 A.D. (95 A.T.) Mika and the Leadership Team of Phoenix want answers. Ishtar gets taken into custody for questioning right after the Warship Horizon lands on Earth's watery surface. His ship and pendant are taken away from him. His inquisition starts.

2147 A.D. (95 A.T.) Three days into questioning,

Ishtar and Peter escape with the apple, pendant, and ship then crash in Anzulla.

2147 A.D. (95 A.T.) Ishtar and Peter return to Phoenix to ask for help. (After Peter had rescued Ish.)

2148 A.D. (96 A.T.) Ishtar and Cian save Phoenix.

AFTERWORD

resemblance to actual persons, living or dead, events, or locales is entirely coincidental.

About the Author

"I found it surprisingly beautiful. In a brutal, horribly uncomfortable sort of way." —Tyrion Lannister to Janos Slynt.

I am a Canadian speculative fiction author, writing in the genres of science fiction, fantasy, and paranormal.

My writing explores who we are, where we come from, and where we are going as a human race on Earth.

I enjoy weaving and exploring questions and subjects about our history and origin by creating new, exciting worlds and characters. My stories are unpredictable, twisted with a dash of humor, and centered on gay characters.

You will question your existence among these worlds and wish you could escape to these places filled with foul-mouthed heroes who struggle and strive to save humankind.

I hope you've discovered something that excites and intrigues you. Please share your thoughts by leaving a review or visiting www.kashelchar.com to contact me or learn about my latest works.